A LOVING WOMAN...
BUT A PERFECT LADY...

He shook a finger at her.

"There you stand in a nice neat coat and skirt looking just the modest sort of girl my mother would have approved of. Why don't you paint your lips pillar-box red and varnish your nails to match? Do you *want* to be an old maid?"

Laura flushed a little.

"No, of course I don't. I just think it's impossible that anyone should fall in love with me."

"Men can fall in love with anything," said Mr. Baldock rudely. "No, young Laura, you just don't want to bother! You want to love—not to be loved—and I daresay you've got something there. To be loved is to carry a heavy burden."

THE BURDEN

Agatha Christie

writing under the name

Mary Westmacott

A DELL BOOK

Published by
DELL PUBLISHING CO., INC.
1 Dag Hammarskjold Plaza
New York, N.Y. 10017

First published 1956 by William Heinemann Ltd.
Dell ® TM 681510, Dell Publishing Co., Inc.

ISBN: 0-440-10863-2

Reprinted by arrangement with
Harold Ober Associates, Inc., New York, New York
Printed in the United States of America
Two previous Dell editions
First printing—May 1983

"For my yoke is easy, and my burden is light."
St. Matthew, Ch. II, v. 30

"Lord, Thy most pointed pleasure take
And stab my spirit broad awake;
Or, Lord, if too obdurate I,
Choose Thou, before that spirit die,
A piercing pain, a killing sin,
And to my dead heart run them in!"
R. L. Stevenson

Contents

Prologue

The church was cold. It was October, too early for the heating to be on. Outside, the sun gave a watery promise of warmth and good cheer, but here within the chill grey stone there was only dampness and a sure foreknowledge of winter.

Laura stood between Nannie, resplendent in crackling collars and cuffs, and Mr. Henson, the curate. The vicar was in bed with mild influenza. Mr. Henson was young and thin, with an Adam's apple and a high nasal voice.

Mrs. Franklin, looking frail and attractive, leant on her husband's arm. He himself stood upright and grave. The birth of his second daughter had not consoled him for the loss of Charles. He had wanted a son. And it seemed now, from what the doctor had said, that there would not be a son. . . .

His eyes went from Laura to the infant in Nannie's arms gurgling happily to itself.

Two daughters . . . Of course Laura was a nice child, a dear child and, as babies go, the new arrival was a splendid specimen, but a man wanted a son.

Charles—Charles, with his fair hair, his way of throwing back his head and laughing. Such an attractive boy, so handsome, so bright, so intelligent. Really a very unusual boy. It seemed a pity that if one of his children had to die, it hadn't been Laura. . . .

His eyes suddenly met those of his elder daughter, eyes that seemed large and tragic in her small pale face, and Franklin flushed guiltily—what had he been thinking of? Suppose the child should guess what had been in his mind. Of course he was devoted to Laura—only—only, she wasn't, she could never be Charles.

Leaning against her husband, her eyes half closed, Angela Franklin was saying to herself:

'My boy—my beautiful boy—my darling. . . . I still can't believe it. Why couldn't it have been Laura?'

She felt no guilt in that thought as it came to her. More ruthless and more honest than her husband, closer to primeval needs, she admitted the simple fact that her second child, a daughter, had never meant, and could never mean to her what her first-born had. Compared with Charles, Laura was an anti-climax—a quiet disappointing child, well-behaved, giving no trouble, but lacking in—what was it?—personality.

She thought again: 'Charles—nothing can ever make up to me for losing Charles.'

She felt the pressure of her husband's hand on her arm, and opened her eyes—she must pay attention to the Service. What a very irritating voice poor Mr. Henson had!

Angela looked with half-amused indulgence at the baby in Nannie's arms—such big solemn words for such a tiny mite.

The baby, who had been sleeping, blinked and opened her eyes. Such dazzling blue eyes—like Charles's eyes—she made a happy gurgling noise.

Angela thought: 'Charles's smile.' A rush of mother love swept over her. Her baby—her own lovely baby. For the first time Charles's death receded into the past.

Angela met Laura's dark sad gaze, and thought with

momentary curiosity: 'I wonder just what that child is thinking?'

Nannie also was conscious of Laura standing quiet and erect beside her.

'Such a quiet little thing,' she thought. 'A bit too quiet for my taste—not natural for any child to be as quiet and well-behaved as she is. There has never been much notice taken of her—maybe not as much as there ought to have been—I wonder now——'

The Reverend Eustace Henson was approaching the moment that always made him nervous. He had not done many christenings. If only the vicar were here. He noticed with approval Laura's grave eyes and serious expression. A well-behaved child. He wondered suddenly what was passing through her mind.

It was as well that neither he, nor Nannie, nor Arthur and Angela Franklin knew.

It wasn't fair. . . .

Oh, it wasn't fair. . . .

Her mother loved this baby sister as much as she loved Charles.

It wasn't *fair*. . . .

She hated the baby—she hated it, hated it, hated it! '*I'd like her to die.*'

Standing by the font, the solemn words of baptism were ringing in her ears—but far more clear, far more real—was the thought translated into words:

'I'd like her to die. . . .'

There was a gentle nudge. Nannie was handing her the baby, whispering:

"Careful, now, take her—steady—and then you hand her to the clergyman." Laura whispered back: "I know."

Baby was in her arms. Laura looked down at her. She thought: 'Supposing I opened my arms and just let her fall—on to the stones. Would it kill her?'

Down on to the stones, so hard and grey—but then babies were so well wrapped up, so—so *padded*. Should she? Dare she?

She hesitated and then the moment was gone—the baby was now in the somewhat nervous arms of the Reverend Eustace Henson, who lacked the practised ease of the vicar. He was asking the names and repeating them after Laura. Shirley, Margaret, Evelyn. . . . The water trickled off the baby's forehead. She did not cry, only gurgled as though an even more delightful thing than usual had happened to her. Gingerly, with inward shrinking, the curate kissed the baby's forehead. The vicar always did that, he knew. With relief he handed the baby back to Nannie.

The christening was over.

part 1

Laura-1929

Chapter one

1

Below the quiet exterior of the child standing beside the font, there raged an ever-growing resentment and misery.

Ever since Charles had died she had hoped . . . Though she had grieved for Charles's death (she had been very fond of Charles), grief had been eclipsed by a tremulous longing and expectation. Naturally, when Charles had been there, Charles with his good looks and his charm and his merry carefree ways, the love had gone to Charles. That, Laura felt, was quite right, was fair. She had always been the quiet, the dull one, the so often unwanted second child that follows too soon upon the first. Her father and mother had been kind to her, affectionate, but it was Charles they had loved.

Once she had overheard her mother say to a visiting friend:

"Laura's a dear child, of course, but rather a dull child."

And she had accepted the justice of that with the honesty of the hopeless. She *was* a dull child. She was small and pale and her hair didn't curl, and the things she said never made people laugh—as they laughed at Charles. She was good and obedient and caused nobody trouble, but she was not and, she thought, never would be, *important.*

Once she had said to Nannie: "Mummy loves Charles more than she loves me. . . ."

Nannie had snapped immediately:

"That's a very silly thing to say and not at all true. Your mother loves both of her children equally—fair as fair can be she is, always. Mothers always love all their children just the same."

"Cats don't," said Laura, reviewing in her mind a recent arrival of kittens.

"Cats are just animals," said Nannie. "And anyway," she added, slightly weakening the magnificent simplicity of her former pronouncement, "God loves you, remember."

Laura accepted the dictum. God loved you—He had to. But even God, Laura thought, probably loved Charles best. . . . Because to have made Charles must be far more satisfactory than to have made her, Laura.

'But of course,' Laura had consoled herself by reflecting, '*I* can love myself best. I can love myself better than Charles or Mummy or Daddy or anyone.'

It was after this that Laura became paler and quieter and more unobtrusive than ever, and was so good and obedient that it made even Nannie uneasy. She confided to the housemaid an uneasy fear that Laura might be 'taken' young.

But it was Charles who died, not Laura.

2

"Why don't you get that child a dog?" Mr. Baldock demanded suddenly of his friend and crony, Laura's father.

Arthur Franklin looked rather astonished, since he was in the middle of an impassioned argument with his friend on the implications of the Reformation.

"What child?" he asked, puzzled.

Mr. Baldock nodded his large head towards a sedate Laura who was propelling herself on a fairy bicycle in and out of the trees on the lawn. It was an unimpassioned performance with no hint of danger or accident about it. Laura was a careful child.

"Why on earth should I?" demanded Mr. Franklin. "Dogs, in my opinion, are a nuisance, always coming in with muddy paws, and ruining the carpets."

"A dog," said Mr. Baldock, in his lecture-room style, which was capable of rousing almost anybody to violent irritation, "has an extraordinary power of bolstering up the human ego. To a dog, the human being who owns him is a god to be worshipped, and not only worshipped but, in our present decadent state of civilisation, also loved.

"The possession of a dog goes to most people's heads. It makes them feel important and powerful."

"Humph," said Mr. Franklin, "and would you call that a good thing?"

"Almost certainly *not*," said Mr. Baldock. "But I have the inveterate weakness of liking to see human beings happy. I'd like to see Laura happy."

"Laura's perfectly happy," said Laura's father. "And anyway she's got a kitten," he added.

"Pah," said Mr. Baldock. "It's not at all the same thing. As you'd realise if you troubled to think. But that's what is wrong with you. You never think. Look at your argument just now about economic conditions at the time of the Reformation. Do you suppose for one moment—"

And they were back at it, hammer and tongs, enjoying themselves a great deal, with Mr. Baldock making the most preposterous and provocative statements.

Yet a vague disquiet lingered somewhere in Arthur Franklin's mind, and that evening, as he came into his wife's room where she was changing for dinner, he said abruptly:

"Laura's quite all right, isn't she? Well and happy and all that?"

His wife turned astonished blue eyes on him, lovely dark cornflower-blue eyes, like the eyes of her son Charles.

"Darling!" she said. "Of course! Laura's always all right. She never even seems to have bilious attacks like most children. I never have to worry about Laura. She's satisfactory in every way. Such a blessing."

A moment later, as she fastened the clasp of her pearls round her neck, she asked suddenly: "Why? Why did you ask about Laura this evening?"

Arthur Franklin said vaguely:

"Oh, just Baldy—something he said."

"Oh, *Baldy!*" Mrs. Franklin's voice held amusement. "You know what *he's* like. He likes starting things."

And on an occasion a few days later when Mr. Baldock had been to lunch, and they came out of the dining-room, encountering Nannie in the hall, Angela Franklin stopped her deliberately and asked in a clear slightly raised voice:

"There's nothing wrong with Miss Laura, is there? She's quite well and happy?"

"Oh yes, Madam." Nannie was positive and slightly affronted. "She's a *very* good little girl, never gives *any* trouble. Not like Master Charles."

"So Charles does give you trouble, does he?" said Mr. Baldock.

Nannie turned to him deferentially.

"He's a regular boy, sir, always up to pranks! He's getting on, you know. He'll soon be going to school. Always high-spirited at this age, they are. And then his digestion is weak, he gets hold of too many sweets without my knowing."

An indulgent smile on her lips and shaking her head, she passed on.

"All the same, she adores him," said Angela Franklin as they went into the drawing-room.

"Obviously," said Mr. Baldock. He added reflectively: "I always have thought women were fools."

"Nannie isn't a fool—very far from it."

"I wasn't thinking of Nannie."

"Me?" Angela gave him a sharp, but not too sharp,

glance, because after all it was Baldy, who was celebrated and eccentric and was allowed a certain licence in rudeness, which was, actually, one of his stock affectations.

"I'm thinking of writing a book on the problem of the second child," said Mr. Baldock.

"Really, Baldy! You don't advocate the only child, do you? I thought that was supposed to be unsound from every point of view."

"Oh! I can see a lot of point in the family of ten. That is, if it was allowed to develop in the legitimate way. Do the household chores, older ones look after the younger ones, and so on. All cogs in the household machine. Mind you, they'd have to be really of some use—not just made to think they were. But nowadays, like fools, we split 'em up and segregate 'em off, each with their own 'age group'! Call it education! Pah! Flat against nature!"

"You and your theories," said Angela indulgently. "But what about the second child?"

"The trouble about the second child," said Mr. Baldock didactically, "is that it's usually an anti-climax. The first child's an adventure. It's frightening and it's painful; the woman's sure she's going to die, and the husband (Arthur here, for example) is equally sure you're going to die. After it's all over, there you are with a small morsel of animate flesh yelling its head off, which has caused two people all kinds of hell to produce! Naturally they value it accordingly! It's new, it's ours, it's wonderful! And then, usually rather too soon, Number Two comes along—all the caboodle over again—not so frightening this time, much more boring. And there it is, it's yours, but it's not a new experience, and since it hasn't cost you so much, it isn't nearly so wonderful."

Angela shrugged her shoulders.

"Bachelors know everything," she murmured ironically. "And isn't that equally true of Number Three and Number Four and all the rest of them?"

"Not quite. I've noticed that there's usually a gap before Number Three. Number Three is often produced because the other two are getting independent, and it would be 'nice to have a baby in the nursery again.' Curious taste; revolting little creatures, but biologically a sound instinct, I suppose. And so they go on, some nice and some nasty, and some bright and some dull, but they pair off and pal up more or less, and finally comes the afterthought which like the first-born gets an undue share of attention."

"And it's all very unfair, is that what you're saying?"

"Exactly. That's the whole point about life, it *is* unfair!"

"And what can one do about it?"

"Nothing."

"Then really, Baldy, I don't see what you're talking about."

"I told Arthur the other day. I'm a soft-hearted chap. I like to see people being happy. I like to make up to people a bit for what they haven't got and can't have. It evens things up a bit. Besides, if you don't—" he paused a moment—"it can be dangerous. . . ."

3

"I do think Baldy talks a lot of nonsense," said Angela pensively to her husband when their guest had departed.

"John Baldock is one of the foremost scholars in this country," said Arthur Franklin with a slight twinkle.

"Oh, I know *that*." Angela was faintly scornful. "I'd be willing to sit in meek adoration if he was laying down the law on Greeks and Romans, or obscure Elizabethan poets. But what can he know about children?"

"Absolutely nothing, I should imagine," said her husband. "By the way, he suggested the other day that we should give Laura a dog."

"A dog? But she's got a kitten."

"According to him, that's not the same thing."

"How very odd . . . I remember him saying once that he disliked dogs."

"I believe he does."

Angela said thoughtfully: "Now Charles, perhaps, ought to have a dog. . . . He looked quite scared the other day when those puppies at the Vicarage rushed at him. I hate to see a boy afraid of dogs. If he had one of his own, it would accustom him to it. He ought to learn to ride, too. I wish he could have a pony of his own. If only we had a paddock!"

"A pony's out of the question, I'm afraid," said Franklin.

In the kitchen, the parlourmaid, Ethel, said to the cook:

"That old Baldock, he's noticed it too."

"Noticed what?"

"Miss Laura. That she isn't long for this world. Asking Nurse about it, they were. Ah, she's got the look, sure enough, no mischief in her, not like Master Charles. You mark my words, *she* won't live to grow up."

But it was Charles who died.

Chapter two

1

Charles died of infantile paralysis. He died at school; two other boys had the disease but recovered.

To Angela Franklin, herself now in a delicate state of health, the blow was so great as to crush her completely. Charles, her beloved, her darling, her handsome merry high-spirited boy.

She lay in her darkened bedroom, staring at the ceiling, unable to weep. And her husband and Laura and the servants crept about the muted house. In the end the doctor advised Arthur Franklin to take his wife abroad.

"Complete change of air and scene. She *must* be roused. Somewhere with good air—mountain air. Switzerland, perhaps."

So the Franklins went off, and Laura remained under the care of Nannie, with daily visits from Miss Weekes, an amiable but uninspiring governess.

To Laura, her parents' absence was a period of pleasure. Technically, she was the mistress of the house! Every morning she 'saw the cook' and ordered meals for the day. Mrs. Brunton, the cook, was fat and good-natured. She curbed the wilder of Laura's suggestions and managed it so that the actual menu was exactly as she herself had planned it. But Laura's sense of importance was not impaired. She missed her parents the less because she was building in her own mind a fantasy for their return.

It was terrible that Charles was dead. Naturally they had loved Charles best—she did not dispute the justice of that, but now—*now*—it was *she* who would enter into Charles's kingdom. It was Laura now who was their only child, the child in whom all their hopes lay and to whom would flow all their affection. She built up scenes in her mind of the day of their return. Her mother's open arms . . .

"Laura, my darling. You're all I have in the world now!"

Affecting scenes, emotional scenes. Scenes that in actual fact were wildly unlike anything Angela or Arthur Franklin were likely to do or say. But to Laura, they were warming and rich in drama, and by slow degrees she began to believe in them so much that they might almost already have happened.

Walking down the lane to the village, she rehearsed conversations: raising her eyebrows, shaking her head, murmuring words and phrases under her breath.

So absorbed was she in this rich feast of emotional imagination, that she failed to observe Mr. Baldock, who was coming towards her from the direction of the village, pushing in front of him a gardening basket on wheels, in which he brought home his purchases.

"Hullo, young Laura."

Laura, rudely jostled out of an affecting drama where her mother had gone blind and she, Laura, had just refused an offer of marriage from a viscount ("I shall never marry. My mother means *everything* to me"), started and blushed.

"Father and mother still away, eh?"

"Yes, they won't be coming back for ten days more."

"I see. Like to come to tea with me tomorrow?"

"Oh, yes."

Laura was elated and excited. Mr. Baldock, who had a Chair at the University fourteen miles away, had a small cottage in the village where he spent the vacations and occasional week-ends. He declined to behave in a social manner, and affronted Bellbury by refusing, usually impolitely, their many invitations. Arthur Franklin was his only friend—it was a friendship of many years standing. John Baldock was not a friendly man. He treated his pupils with such ruthlessness and irony that the best of them were goaded into distinguishing themselves, and the rest perished by the wayside. He had written several large and abstruse volumes on obscure phases of history, written in such a way that very few people could understand what he was driving at. Mild appeals from his publishers to write in a more readable fashion were turned down with a savage glee, Mr. Baldock pointing out that the people who could appreciate his books were the only readers of them who were worthwhile! He was particularly rude to women, which enchanted many of them so much that they were always coming back for more. A man of savage prejudices, and over-riding arrogance, he had an unexpectedly kindly heart which was always betraying his principles.

Laura knew that to be asked to tea with Mr. Baldock was an honour, and preened herself accordingly. She turned up neatly dressed, brushed, and washed, but nevertheless with an underlying apprehension, for Mr. Baldock was an alarming man.

Mr. Baldock's housekeeper showed her into the library, where Mr. Baldock raised his head, and stared at her.

"Hullo," said Mr. Baldock. "What are you doing here?"

"You asked me to tea," said Laura.

Mr. Baldock looked at her in a considering manner. Laura looked back at him. It was a grave, polite look that successfully concealed her inner uncertainty.

"So I did," said Mr. Baldock, rubbing his nose. "Hm . . . yes, so I did. Can't think why. Well, you'd better sit down."

"Where?" said Laura.

The question was highly pertinent. The library into which Laura had been shown was a room lined with bookshelves to the ceiling. All the shelves were wedged tight with books, but there still existed large numbers of books which could find no places in the shelves, and these were piled in great heaps on the floor and on tables, and also occupied the chairs.

Mr. Baldock looked vexed.

"I suppose we'll have to do something about it," he said grudgingly.

He selected an armchair that was slightly less encumbered than the others and, with many grunts and puffs, lowered two armsful of dusty tomes to the floor.

"There you are," he said, beating his hands together to rid them of dust. As a result, he sneezed violently.

"Doesn't anyone ever dust in here?" Laura asked, as she sat down sedately.

"Not if they value their lives!" said Mr. Baldock. "But mind you, it's a hard fight. Nothing a woman likes better than to come barging in flicking a great yellow duster, and armed with tins of greasy stuff smelling of turpentine or worse. Picking up all my books, and arranging them in piles, by size as likely as not, no concern for the subject matter! Then she starts an evil-looking machine, that wheezes and hums, and out she goes finally, as pleased as Punch, having left the place in such a state that you can't put your hand on a thing you want for at least a month. Women! What the Lord God thought he was doing when he created woman, I can't imagine. I daresay He thought Adam was looking a little too cocky and pleased with himself; Lord of the Universe, and naming the animals and all that. Thought he needed taking down a peg or two. Daresay that was true enough. But creating woman was going a bit far. Look where it landed the poor chap! Slap in the middle of Original Sin."

"I'm sorry," said Laura apologetically.

"What do you mean, sorry?"

"That you feel like that about women, because I suppose I'm a woman."

"Not yet you're not, thank goodness," said Mr. Baldock. "Not for a long while yet. It's got to come, of course, but no point in looking ahead towards unpleasant things. And by the way, I *hadn't* forgotten that you were coming to tea to-day. Not for a moment! I just pretended that I had for a reason of my own."

"What reason?"

"Well—" Mr. Baldock rubbed his nose again. "For one thing I wanted to see what you'd say." He nodded his head. "You came through that one very well. Very well indeed. . . ."

Laura stared at him uncomprehendingly.

"I had another reason. If you and I are going to be friends, and it rather looks as though things are tending that way, then you've got to accept me as I am—a rude, ungracious old curmudgeon. See? No good expecting pretty speeches. 'Dear child—so pleased to see you— been looking forward to your coming.' "

Mr. Baldock repeated these last phrases in a high falsetto tone of unmitigated contempt. A ripple passed over Laura's grave face. She laughed.

"That would be funny," she said.

"It would indeed. Very funny."

Laura's gravity returned. She looked at him speculatively.

"Do you think we *are* going to be friends?" she inquired.

"It's a matter for mutual agreement. Do you care for the idea?"

Laura considered.

"It seems—a little odd," she said dubiously. "I mean, friends are usually children who come and play games with you."

"You won't find me playing 'Here We Go Round the Mulberry Bush,' and don't you think it!"

"That's only for babies," said Laura reprovingly.

"Our friendship would be definitely on an intellectual plane," said Mr. Baldock.

Laura looked pleased.

"I don't really know quite what that means," she said, "but I think I like the sound of it."

"It means," said Mr. Baldock, "that when we meet we discuss subjects which are of interest to both of us."

"What kind of subjects?"

"Well—food, for instance. I'm fond of food. I expect you are, too. But as I'm sixty-odd, and you're—what is it, ten?—I've no doubt that our ideas on the matter will differ. That's interesting. Then there will be other things —colours—flowers—animals—English history."

"You mean things like Henry the Eighth's wives?"

"Exactly. Mention Henry the Eighth to nine people out of ten, and they'll come back at you with his wives. It's an insult to a man who was called the Fairest Prince in Christendom, and who was a statesman of the first order of craftiness, to remember him only by his matrimonial efforts to get a legitimate male heir. His wretched wives are of no importance *whatever* historically."

"Well, *I* think his wives were very important."

"There you are!" said Mr. Baldock. "Discussion."

"I should like to have been Jane Seymour."

"Now why her?"

"She died," said Laura ecstatically.

"So did Nan Bullen and Katherine Howard."

"They were executed. Jane was only married to him for a year, and she had a baby and died, and everyone must have been terribly sorry."

"Well—that's a point of view. Come in the other room and see if we've got anything for tea."

2

"It's a wonderful tea," said Laura ecstatically.

Her eyes roamed over currant buns, jam roll, éclairs, cucumber sandwiches, chocolate biscuits and a large indigestible-looking rich black plum cake.

She gave a sudden little giggle.

"You *did* expect me," she said. "Unless—do you have a tea like this every day?"

"God forbid," said Mr. Baldock.

They sat down companionably. Mr. Baldock had six cucumber sandwiches, and Laura had four éclairs, and a selection of everything else.

"Got a good appetite, I'm glad to see, young Laura," said Mr. Baldock appreciatively as they finished.

"I'm always hungry," said Laura, "and I'm hardly ever sick. Charles used to be sick."

"Hm . . . Charles. I suppose you miss Charles a lot?"

"Oh yes, I do. I do, *really*."

Mr. Baldock's bushy grey eyebrows rose.

"All right. All right. Who says you don't miss him?"

"Nobody. And I do—I really *do*."

He nodded gravely in answer to her earnestness, and watched her. He was wondering.

"It was terribly sad, his dying like that." Laura's voice unconsciously reproduced the tones of another voice, some adult voice, which had originally uttered the phrase.

"Yes, very sad."

"Terribly sad for Mummy and Daddy. Now—I'm all they've got in the world."

"So that's it?"

She looked at him uncomprehendingly.

She had gone into her private dream world. *"Laura, my darling. You're all I have—my only child—my treasure. . . ."*

"Bad butter," said Mr. Baldock. It was one of his expressions of perturbation. "Bad butter! Bad butter!" He shook his head vexedly.

"Come out in the garden, Laura," he said. "We'll have a look at the roses. Tell me what you do with yourself all day."

"Well, in the morning Miss Weekes comes and we do lessons."

"That old Tabby!"

"Don't you like her?"

"She's got Girton written all over her. Mind you never go to Girton, Laura!"

"What's Girton?"

"It's a woman's college. At Cambridge. Makes my flesh creep when I think about it!"

"I'm going to boarding school when I'm twelve."

"Sinks of iniquity, boarding schools!"

"Don't you think I'll like it?"

"I daresay you'll *like* it all right. That's just the danger! Hacking other girls' ankles with a hockey stick, coming home with a crush on the music mistress, going on to Girton or Somerville as likely as not. Oh well, we've got a couple of years still, before the worst happens. Let's make the most of it. What are you going to do when you grow up? I suppose you've got some notions about it?"

"I did think that I might go and nurse lepers—"

"Well, that's harmless enough. Don't bring one home and put him in your husband's bed, though. St. Elizabeth of Hungary did that. Most misguided zeal. A Saint of God, no doubt, but a very inconsiderate wife."

"I shall never marry," said Laura in a voice of renunciation.

"No? Oh, I think I should marry if I were you. Old maids are worse than married women in my opinion. Hard luck on some man, of course, but I daresay you'd make a better wife than many."

"It wouldn't be right. I must look after Mummy and Daddy in their old age. They've got nobody but me."

"They've got a cook and a house-parlourmaid and a gardener, and a good income, and plenty of friends. *They'll* be all right. Parents have to put up with their children leaving them when the time comes. Great relief sometimes." He stopped abruptly by a bed of roses. "Here are my roses. Like 'em?"

"They're beautiful," said Laura politely.

"On the whole," said Mr. Baldock, "I prefer them to human beings. They don't last as long for one thing."

Then he took Laura firmly by the hand.

"Good-bye, Laura," he said. "You've got to be going now. Friendship should never be strained too far. I've enjoyed having you to tea."

"Good-bye, Mr. Baldock. Thank you for having me. I've enjoyed myself very much."

The polite slogan slipped from her lips in a glib fashion. Laura was a well-brought-up child.

"That's right," said Mr. Baldock, patting her amicably on the shoulder. "Always say your piece. It's courtesy, and knowing the right passwords that makes the wheels go round. When you come to my age, you can say what you like."

Laura smiled at him and passed through the iron gate he was holding open for her. Then she turned and hesitated.

"Well, what is it?"

"Is it really settled now? About our being friends, I mean?"

Mr. Baldock rubbed his nose.

"Yes," he said with a sigh. "Yes, I think so."

"I hope you don't mind very much?" Laura asked anxiously.

"Not too much. . . . I've got to get used to the idea, mind."

"Yes, of course. *I've* got to get used to it, too. But I think—I think—it's going to be nice. Good-bye."

"Good-bye."

Mr. Baldock looked after her retreating figure, and muttered to himself fiercely: "*Now* look what you've let yourself in for, you old fool!"

He retraced his steps to the house, and was met by his housekeeper Mrs. Rouse.

"Has the little girl gone?"

"Yes, she's gone."

"Oh dear, she didn't stay very long, did she?"

"Quite long enough," said Mr. Baldock. "Children and one's social inferiors never know when to say good-bye. One has to say it for them."

"Well!" said Mrs. Rouse, gazing after him indignantly as he walked past her.

"Good-night," said Mr. Baldock. "I'm going into my library, and I don't want to be disturbed again."

"About supper—"

"Anything you please." Mr. Baldock waved an arm. "And take away all that sweet stuff, and finish it up, or give it to the cat."

"Oh, thank you, sir. My little niece—"

"Your niece, or the cat, or *anyone.*"

He went into the library and shut the door.

"Well!" said Mrs. Rouse again. "Of all the crusty old bachelors! But there, I understand his ways! It's not everyone that would."

Laura went home with a pleasing feeling of importance.

She popped her head through the kitchen window where Ethel, the house-parlourmaid, was struggling with the intricacies of a crochet pattern.

"Ethel," said Laura. "I've got a Friend."

"Yes, dearie," said Ethel, murmuring to herself under her breath. "Five chain, twice into the next stitch, eight chain—"

"I *have* got a Friend." Laura stressed the information.

Ethel was still murmuring:

"Five double crochet, and then three times into the next—but that makes it come out wrong at the end—now where have I slipped up?"

"I've got a *Friend,*" shouted Laura, maddened by the lack of comprehension displayed by her confidante.

Ethel looked up, startled.

"Well, rub it, dearie, rub it," she said vaguely.

Laura turned away in disgust.

Chapter three

1

Angela Franklin had dreaded returning home but, when the time came, she found it not half so bad as she had feared.

As they drove up to the door, she said to her husband:

"There's Laura waiting for us on the steps. She looks quite excited."

And, jumping out as the car drew up, she folded her arms affectionately round her daughter and cried:

"Laura darling. It's lovely to see you. Have you missed us a lot?"

Laura said conscientiously:

"Not very much. I've been very busy. But I've made you a raffia mat."

Swiftly there swept over Angela's mind a sudden remembrance of Charles—of the way he would tear across the grass, flinging himself upon her, hugging her. "Mummy, Mummy, Mummy!"

How horribly it hurt—remembering.

She pushed aside memories, smiled at Laura and said:

"A raffia mat? How nice, darling."

Arthur Franklin tweaked his daughter's hair.

"I believe you've grown, Puss."

They all went into the house.

What it was Laura had expected, she did not know.

Here were Mummy and Daddy home, and pleased to see her, making a fuss of her, asking her questions. It wasn't *they* who were wrong, it was herself. She wasn't—she wasn't—what wasn't she?

She herself hadn't said the things or looked or even felt as she had thought she would.

It wasn't the way she had planned it. She hadn't—really—taken Charles's place. There was something missing with her, Laura. But it would be different tomorrow, she told herself, or if not tomorrow, then the next day, or the day after. The heart of the house, Laura said to herself, suddenly recalling a phrase that had taken her fancy from an old-fashioned children's book she had come across in the attic.

That was what she was now, surely, the heart of the house.

Unfortunate that she should feel herself, with a deep inner misgiving, to be just Laura as usual.

Just Laura. . . .

2

"Baldy seems to have taken quite a fancy to Laura," said Angela. "Fancy, he asked her to tea with him while we were away."

Arthur said he'd like very much to know what they had talked about.

"I think," said Angela after a moment or two, "that we ought to *tell* Laura. I mean, if we don't, she'll hear something—the servants or someone. After all, she's too old for gooseberry bushes and all that kind of thing."

She was lying in a long basket chair under the cedar tree. She turned her head now towards her husband in his deck chair.

The lines of suffering still showed in her face. The life she was carrying had not yet succeeded in blurring the sense of loss.

"It's going to be a boy," said Arthur Franklin. "I know it's going to be a boy."

Angela smiled, and shook her head.

"No use building on it," she said.

"I tell you, Angela, I know."

He was positive—quite positive.

A boy like Charles, another Charles, laughing, blue-eyed, mischievous, affectionate.

Angela thought: 'It may be another boy—but it won't be Charles.'

"I expect we shall be just as pleased with a girl, however," said Arthur, not very convincingly.

"Arthur, you know you want a son!"

"Yes," he sighed, "I'd like a son."

A man wanted a son—needed a son. Daughters—it wasn't the same thing.

Obscurely moved by some consciousness of guilt, he said:

"Laura's really a dear little thing."

Angela agreed sincerely.

"I know. So good and quiet and helpful. We shall miss her when she goes to school."

She added: "That's partly why I hope it won't be a girl. Laura might be a teeny bit jealous of a baby sister—not that she'd have any need to be."

"Of course not."

"But children are sometimes—it's quite natural; that's why I think we ought to tell her, prepare her."

And so it was that Angela Franklin said to her daughter:

"How would you like a little baby brother?"

"Or sister?" she added rather belatedly.

Laura stared at her. The words did not seem to make sense. She was puzzled. She did not understand.

Angela said gently: "You see, darling, I'm going to have a baby . . . next September. It will be nice, won't it?"

She was a little disturbed when Laura, murmuring

something incoherent, backed away, her face crimsoning with an emotion that her mother did not understand.

Angela Franklin felt worried.

"I wonder," she said to her husband. "Perhaps we've been wrong? I've never actually told her anything—about —about *things,* I mean. Perhaps she hadn't any idea . . ."

Arthur Franklin said that considering that the production of kittens that went on in the house was something astronomical, it was hardly likely that Laura was completely unacquainted with the facts of life.

"Yes, but perhaps she thinks people are different. It may have been a shock to her."

It had been a shock to Laura, though not in any biological sense. It was simply that the idea that her mother would have another child had never occurred to Laura. She had seen the whole pattern as simple and straightforward. Charles was dead, and she was her parents' only child. She was, as she had phrased it to herself, *'all they had in the world.'*

And now—now—there was to be another Charles.

She never doubted, any more than Arthur and Angela secretly doubted, that the baby would be a boy.

Desolation struck through to her.

For a long time Laura sat huddled upon the edge of a cucumber-frame, while she wrestled with disaster.

Then she made up her mind. She got up, walked down the drive and along the road to Mr. Baldock's house.

Mr. Baldock, grinding his teeth and snorting with venom, was penning a really vitriolic review for a learned journal of a fellow historian's life work.

He turned a ferocious face to the door, as Mrs. Rouse, giving a perfunctory knock and pushing it open, announced:

"Here's little Miss Laura for you."

"Oh," said Mr. Baldock, checked on the verge of a tremendous flood of invective. "So it's you."

He was disconcerted. A fine thing it would be if the child was going to trot along here at any odd moment.

He hadn't bargained for *that*. Drat all children! Give them an inch and they took an ell. He didn't like children, anyway. He never had.

His disconcerted gaze met Laura's. There was no apology in Laura's look. It was grave, deeply troubled, but quite confident in a divine right to be where she was. She made no polite remarks of an introductory nature.

"I thought I'd come and tell you," she said, "that I'm going to have a baby brother."

"Oh," said Mr. Baldock, taken aback.

"We-ell : . ." he said, playing for time. Laura's face was white and expressionless. "That's news, isn't it?" He paused. "Are you pleased?"

"No," said Laura. "I don't think I am."

"Beastly things, babies," agreed Mr. Baldock sympathetically. "No teeth and no hair, and yell their heads off. Their mothers like them, of course, have to—or the poor little brutes would never get looked after, or grow up. But you won't find it so bad when it's three or four," he added encouragingly. "Almost as good as a kitten or a puppy by then."

"Charles died," said Laura. "Do you think it's likely that my new baby brother may die too?"

He shot her a keen glance, then said firmly:

"Shouldn't think so for a moment," and added: "Lightning never strikes twice."

"Cook says that," said Laura. "It means the same thing doesn't happen twice?"

"Quite right."

"Charles—" began Laura, and stopped.

Again Mr. Baldock's glance swept over her quickly.

"No reason it should be a baby brother," he said. "Just as likely to be a baby sister."

"Mummy seems to think it will be a brother."

"Shouldn't go by that if I were you. She wouldn't be the first woman to think wrong."

Laura's face brightened suddenly.

"There was Jehoshaphat," she said. "Dulcibella's last

kitten. He's turned out to be a girl after all. Cook calls him Josephine now," she added.

"There you are," said Mr. Baldock encouragingly. "I'm not a betting man, but I'd put my money on its being a girl myself."

"Would you?" said Laura fervently.

She smiled at him, a grateful and unexpectedly lovely smile that gave Mr. Baldock quite a shock.

"Thank you," she said. "I'll go now." She added politely: "I hope I haven't interrupted your work?"

"It's quite all right," said Mr. Baldock. "I'm always glad to see you if it's about something important. I know you wouldn't barge in here just to chatter."

"Of course I wouldn't," said Laura earnestly.

She withdrew, closing the door carefully behind her.

The conversation had cheered her considerably. Mr. Baldock, she knew, was a very clever man.

"He's much more likely to be right than Mummy," she thought to herself.

A baby sister? Yes, she could face the thought of a sister. A sister would only be another Laura—an inferior Laura. A Laura lacking teeth and hair, and any kind of sense.

3

As she emerged from the kindly haze of the anaesthetic, Angela's cornflower-blue eyes asked the eager question that her lips were almost afraid to form.

"Is it—all right—is it—?"

The nurse spoke glibly and briskly after the manner of nurses.

"You've got a lovely daughter, Mrs. Franklin."

"A daughter—a daughter . . ." The blue eyes closed again.

Disappointment surged through her. She had been so sure—so sure. . . . Only a second Laura . . .

The old tearing pain of her loss reawakened. Charles,

her handsome laughing Charles. Her boy, her son . . .

Downstairs, Cook was saying briskly:

"Well, Miss Laura. You've got a little sister, what do you think of *that?*"

Laura replied sedately to Cook:

"I knew I'd have a sister. Mr. Baldock said so."

"An old bachelor like him, what should he know?"

"He's a very clever man," said Laura.

Angela was rather slow to regain her full strength. Arthur Franklin was worried about his wife. The baby was a month old when he spoke to Angela rather hesitatingly.

"Does it matter so much? That it's a girl, I mean, and not a boy?"

"No, of course not. Not really. Only—I'd felt so sure."

"Even if it had been a boy, it wouldn't have been Charles, you know?"

"No. No, of course not."

The nurse entered the room, carrying the baby.

"Here we are," she said. "Such a lovely girl now. Going to your Mumsie-wumsie, aren't you?"

Angela held the baby slackly and eyed the nurse with dislike as the latter went out of the room.

"What idiotic things these women say," she muttered crossly.

Arthur laughed.

"Laura darling, get me that cushion," said Angela.

Laura brought it to her, and stood by as Angela arranged the baby more comfortably. Laura felt comfortably mature and important. The baby was only a silly little thing. It was she, Laura, on whom her mother relied.

It was chilly this evening. The fire that burned in the grate was pleasant. The baby crowed and gurgled happily.

Angela looked down into the dark blue eyes, and a mouth that seemed already to be able to smile. She looked down, with sudden shock, into Charles's eyes. Charles as a baby. She had almost forgotten him at that age.

Love rushed blindingly through her veins. *Her* baby,

her darling. How could she have been so cold, so unloving to this adorable creature? How could she have been so blind? A gay beautiful child, like Charles.

"My sweet," she murmured. "My precious, my darling."

She bent over the child in an abandonment of love. She was oblivious of Laura standing watching her. She did not notice as Laura crept quietly out of the room.

But perhaps a vague uneasiness made her say to Arthur:

"Mary Wells can't be here for the christening. Shall we let Laura be proxy godmother? It would please her, I think."

Chapter four

1

"Enjoy the christening?" asked Mr. Baldock.

"No," said Laura.

"Cold in that church, I expect," said Mr. Baldock. "Nice font though," he added. "Norman—black Tournai marble."

Laura was unmoved by the information.

She was busy formulating a question:

"May I ask you something, Mr. Baldock?"

"Of course."

"Is it wrong to pray for anyone to die?"

Mr. Baldock gave her a swift sideways look.

"In my view," he said, "it would be unpardonable interference."

"Interference?"

"Well, the Almighty is running the show, isn't He? What do you want to stick *your* fingers into the machinery for? What business is it of yours?"

"I don't see that it would matter to God very much. When a baby has been christened and everything, it goes to heaven, doesn't it?"

"Don't see where else it could go," admitted Mr. Baldock.

"And God is fond of children. The Bible says so. So He'd be pleased to see it."

Mr. Baldock took a short turn up and down the room. He was seriously upset, and didn't want to show it.

"Look here, Laura," he said at last. "You've got—you've simply *got* to mind your own business."

"But perhaps it is my business."

"No, it isn't. *Nothing's* your business but *yourself*. Pray what you like about yourself. Ask for blue ears, or a diamond tiara, or to grow up and win a beauty competition. The worst that can happen to you is that the answer to your prayer might be 'Yes'."

Laura looked at him uncomprehendingly.

"I mean it," said Mr. Baldock.

Laura thanked him politely, and said she must be going home now.

When she had gone, Mr. Baldock rubbed his chin, scratched his head, picked his nose, and absent-mindedly wrote a review of a mortal enemy's book simply dripping with milk and honey.

Laura walked back home, thinking deeply.

As she passed the small Roman Catholic church, she hesitated. A daily woman who came in to help in the kitchen was a Catholic, and stray scraps of her conversation came back to Laura, who had listened to them with the fascination accorded to something rare and strange, and also forbidden. For Nannie, a staunch chapel-goer, held very strong views about what she referred to as the Scarlet Woman. Who or what the Scarlet Woman was, Laura had no idea, except that she had some undefined connection with Babylon.

But what came to her mind now was Molly's chat of praying for her Intention—a candle had entered into it in some way. Laura hesitated a little longer, drew a deep breath, looked up and down the road, and slipped into the porch.

The church was small and rather dark, and did not smell at all like the parish church where Laura went every Sunday. There was no sign of the Scarlet Woman, but there was a plaster figure of a lady in a blue cloak, with a tray in front of her, and wire loops in which candles were burning. Near-by was a supply of fresh candles, and a box with a slot for money.

Laura hesitated for some time. Her theological ideas were confused and limited. God she knew, God who was committed to loving her by the fact that He was God. There was also the Devil, with horns and a tail, and a specialist in temptation. But the Scarlet Woman appeared to occupy an in-between status. The Lady in the Blue Cloak looked beneficent, and as though she might deal with Intentions in a favourable manner.

Laura drew a deep sigh and fumbled in her pocket where reposed, as yet untouched, her weekly sixpence of pocket money.

She pushed it into the slit and heard it drop with a slight pang. Gone irrevocably! Then she took a candle, lit it, and put it into the wire holder. She spoke in a low polite voice.

"This is my Intention. Please let baby go to Heaven." She added:

"As soon as you possibly can, please."

She stood there for a moment. The candles burned, the Lady in the Blue Cloak continued to look beneficent. Laura had for a moment or two a feeling of emptiness. Then, frowning a little, she left the church and walked home.

On the terrace was the baby's pram. Laura came up to it and stood beside it, looking down on the sleeping infant.

As she looked, the fair downy head stirred, the eyelids opened, and blue eyes looked up at Laura with a wide un-focused stare.

"You're going to Heaven soon," Laura told her sister. "It's lovely in Heaven," she added coaxingly. "All golden and precious stones."

"And harps," she added, after a minute. "And lots of angels with real feathery wings. It's much nicer than here."

She thought of something else.

"You'll see Charles," she said. "Think of that! You'll see Charles."

Angela Franklin came out of the drawing-room window.

"Hullo, Laura," she said. "Are you talking to baby?"

She bent over the pram. "Hullo, my sweetie. Was it awake, then?"

Arthur Franklin, following his wife out on to the terrace, said:

"Why do women have to talk such nonsense to babies? Eh, Laura? Don't you think it's odd?"

"I don't think it's nonsense," said Laura.

"Don't you? What do you think it is, then?" He smiled at her teasingly.

"I think it's love," said Laura.

He was a little taken aback.

Laura, he thought, was an odd kid. Difficult to know what went on behind that straight, unemotional gaze.

"I must get a piece of netting, muslin or something," said Angela. "To put over the pram when it's out here. I'm always so afraid of a cat jumping up and lying on her face and suffocating her. We've got too many cats about the place."

"Bah," said her husband. "That's one of those old wives' tales. I don't believe a cat has ever suffocated a baby."

"Oh, they have, Arthur. You read about it quite often in the paper."

"That's no guarantee of truth."

"Anyway, I shall get some netting, and I must tell Nannie to look out of the window from time to time and see that she's all right. Oh dear, I wish our own nanny hadn't had to go to her dying sister. This new young nanny—I don't really feel happy about her."

"Why not? She seems a nice enough girl. Devoted to baby and good references and all that."

"Oh yes, I know. She *seems* all right. But there's something . . . There's that gap of a year and a half in her references."

"She went home to nurse her mother."

"That's what they always say! And it's the sort of thing you can't check. It might have been for some reason she doesn't want us to know about."

"Got into trouble, you mean?"

Angela threw him a warning glance, indicating Laura.

"Do be careful, Arthur. No, I don't mean that. I mean—"

"What do you mean, darling?"

"I don't really know," said Angela slowly. "It's just— sometimes when I'm talking to her I feel that there's something she's anxious we shouldn't find out."

"Wanted by the police?"

"Arthur! That's a very silly joke."

Laura walked gently away. She was an intelligent child and she perceived quite plainly that they, her father and mother, would like to talk about Nannie unhampered by her presence. She herself was not interested in the new nanny; a pale, dark-haired, soft-spoken girl, who showed herself kindly to Laura, though plainly quite uninterested by her.

Laura was thinking of the Lady with the Blue Cloak.

2

"Come *on,* Josephine," said Laura crossly.

Josephine, late Jehoshaphat, though not actively re-sisting, was displaying all the signs of passive resistance. Disturbed in a delicious sleep against the side of the greenhouse, she had been half dragged, half carried by Laura, out of the kitchen-garden and round the house to the terrace.

"There!" Laura plopped Josephine down. A few feet away, the baby's pram stood on the gravel.

Laura walked slowly away across the lawn. As she

reached the big lime tree, she turned her head.

Josephine, her tail lashing from time to time, in indignant memory, began to wash her stomach, sticking out what seemed a disproportionately long hind leg. That part of her toilet completed, she yawned and looked round her at her surroundings. Then she began half-heartedly to wash behind the ears, thought better of it, yawned again, and finally got up and walked slowly and meditatively away, and round the corner of the house.

Laura followed her, picked her up determinedly, and lugged her back again. Josephine gave Laura a look and sat there lashing her tail. As soon as Laura had got back to the tree, Josephine once more got up, yawned, stretched, and walked off. Laura brought her back again, remonstrating as she did so.

"It's sunny here, Josephine. It's *nice!*"

Nothing could be clearer than that Josephine disagreed with this statement. She was now in a very bad temper indeed, lashing her tail, and flattening back her ears.

"Hullo, young Laura."

Laura started and turned. Mr. Baldock stood behind her. She had not heard or noticed his slow progress across the lawn. Josephine, profiting by Laura's momentary inattention, darted to a tree and ran up it, pausing on a branch to look down on them with an air of malicious satisfaction.

"That's where cats have the advantage over human beings," said Mr. Baldock. "When they want to get away from people they can climb a tree. The nearest we can get to that is to shut ourselves in the lavatory."

Laura looked slightly shocked. Lavatories came into the category of things which Nannie (the late Nannie) had said 'little ladies don't talk about.'

"But one has to come out," said Mr. Baldock, "if for no other reason than because other people want to come in. Now that cat of yours will probably stay up that tree for a couple of hours."

Immediately Josephine demonstrated the general unpredictability of cats by coming down with a rush, crossing towards them, and proceeding to rub herself to and fro against Mr. Baldock's trousers, purring loudly.

"Here," she seemed to say, "is exactly what I have been waiting for."

"Hullo, Baldy." Angela came out of the window. "Are you paying your respects to the latest arrival? Oh dear, these *cats*. Laura dear, do take Josephine away. Put her in the kitchen. I haven't got that netting yet. Arthur laughs at me, but cats do jump up and sleep on babies' chests and smother them. I don't want the cats to get the habit of coming round to the terrace."

As Laura went off carrying Josephine, Mr. Baldock sent a considering gaze after her.

After lunch, Arthur Franklin drew his friend into the study.

"There's an article here——" he began.

Mr. Baldock interrupted him, without ceremony and forthrightly, as was his custom.

"Just a minute. I've got something *I* want to say. Why don't you send that child to school?"

"Laura? That is the idea——after Christmas, I believe. When she's eleven."

"Don't wait for that. Do it now."

"It would be mid-term. And, anyway, Miss Weekes is quite——"

Mr. Baldock said what he thought of Miss Weekes with relish.

"Laura doesn't want instruction from a desiccated blue-stocking, however bulging with brains," he said. "She wants distraction, other girls, a different set of troubles if you like. Otherwise, for all you know, you may have a tragedy."

"A tragedy? What sort of tragedy?"

"A couple of nice little boys the other day took their baby sister out of the pram and threw her in the river. The baby made too much work for Mummy, they said.

They had quite genuinely made themselves believe it, I imagine."

Arthur Franklin stared at him.

"Jealousy, you mean?"

"Jealousy."

"My dear Baldy, Laura's not a jealous child. Never has been."

"How do you know? Jealousy eats inward."

"She's never shown any sign of it. She's a very sweet, gentle child, but without any very strong feelings, I should say."

"*You'd* say!" Mr. Baldock snorted. "If you ask me, you and Angela don't know the first thing about your own child."

Arthur Franklin smiled good-temperedly. He was used to Baldy.

"We'll keep an eye on the baby," he said, "if that's what's worrying you. I'll give Angela a hint to be careful. Tell her not to make too much fuss of the newcomer, and a bit more of Laura. That ought to meet the case." He added with a hint of curiosity: "I've always wondered just what it is you see in Laura. She—"

"There's promise there of a very rare and unusual spirit," said Mr. Baldock. "At least so I think."

"Well—I'll speak to Angela—but she'll only laugh."

But Angela, rather to her husband's surprise, did not laugh.

"There's something in what he says, you know. Child psychologists all agree that jealousy over a new baby is natural and almost inevitable. Though frankly *I* haven't seen any signs of it in Laura. She's a placid child, and it isn't as though she were wildly attached to *me* or anything like that. I must try and show her that I depend upon her."

And so, when about a week later, she and her husband were going for a week-end visit to some old friends, Angela talked to Laura.

"You'll take good care of baby, won't you, Laura, while we're away? It's nice to feel I'm leaving you here to keep an eye on everything. Nannie hasn't been here very long, you see."

Her mother's words pleased Laura. They made her feel old and important. Her small pale face brightened.

Unfortunately, the good effect was destroyed almost immediately by a conversation between Nannie and Ethel in the nursery, which she happened to overhear.

"Lovely baby, isn't she?' said Ethel, poking the infant with a crudely affectionate finger. "There's a little ducksie-wucksie. Seems funny Miss Laura's always been such a plain little thing. Don't wonder her pa and ma never took to her, as they took to Master Charles and this one. Miss Laura's a nice little thing, but you can't say more than that."

That evening Laura knelt by her bed and prayed.

The Lady with the Blue Cloak had taken no notice of her Intention. Laura was going to headquarters.

"Please, God," she prayed, *"let baby die and go to Heaven soon. Very soon."*

She got into bed and lay down. Her heart beat, and she felt guilty and wicked. She had done what Mr. Baldock had told her not to do, and Mr. Baldock was a very wise man. She had had no feeling of guilt about her candle to the Lady in the Blue Cloak—possibly because she had never really had much hope of any result. And she could see no harm in just bringing Josephine on to the terrace. She wouldn't have put Josephine actually on to the pram. That, she knew, *would* have been wicked. But if Josephine, of her own accord . . . ?

To-night, however, she had crossed the Rubicon. God was all-powerful. . . .

Shivering a little, Laura fell asleep.

Chapter five

1

Angela and Arthur Franklin drove away in the car.

Up in the nursery, the new nanny, Gwyneth Jones, was putting the baby to bed.

She was uneasy to-night. There had been certain feelings, portents, lately, and to-night—

"I'm just imagining it," she said to herself. "Fancy! That's all it is."

Hadn't the doctor told her that it was quite possible she might never have another fit?

She'd had them as a child, and then never a sign of anything of the kind until that terrible day . . .

Teething convulsions, her aunt had called those childhood seizures. But the doctor had used another name, had said plainly and without subterfuge what the malady was. And he had said, quite definitely: "You mustn't take a place with a baby or children. It wouldn't be safe."

But she'd paid for that expensive training. It was her trade—what she knew how to do—certificates and all—well paid—and she loved looking after babies. A year had gone by, and there had been no recurrence of trouble. It was all nonsense, the doctor frightening her like that.

So she'd written to the bureau—a different bureau, and she'd soon got a place, and she was happy here, and the baby was a little love.

She put the baby into her cot and went downstairs for

her supper. She awoke in the night with a sense of uneasiness, almost terror. She thought:

'I'll make myself a drop of hot milk. It will calm me down.'

She lit the spirit lamp and carried it to the table near the window.

There was no final warning. She went down like a stone, lying there on the floor, jerking and twisting. The spirit lamp fell to the floor, and the flame from it ran across the carpet and reached the end of the muslin curtains.

2

Laura woke up suddenly.

She had been dreaming—a bad dream—though she couldn't remember the details of it. Something chasing her, something—but she was safe now, in her own bed, at home.

She felt for the lamp by her bedside, and turned it on, and looked at her own little clock. Twelve o'clock. Midnight.

She sat up in bed, feeling a curious reluctance to turn out the light again.

She listened. What a queer creaking noise. . . . 'Burglars perhaps,' thought Laura, who like most children was perpetually suspecting burglars. She got out of bed and went to the door, opened it a little way, and peered cautiously out. Everything was dark and quiet.

But there was a smell, a funny smoky smell, Laura sniffed experimentally. She went across the landing and opened the door that led to the servants' quarters. Nothing.

She crossed to the other side of the landing, where a door shut off a short passage leading to the nursery and the nursery bathroom.

Then she shrank back, appalled. Great wreaths of smoke came curling towards her.

"It's on fire. The house is on fire!"

Laura screamed, rushed to the servants' wing, and called:

"Fire! The house is on fire!"

She could never remember clearly what came after. Cook and Ethel—Ethel running downstairs to telephone, Cook opening that door across the landing and being driven back by the smoke, Cook soothing her with: "It'll be all right." Incoherent murmurs: "The engine will come—they'll get them out through the window—don't you worry, my dear."

But it would not be all right. Laura knew.

She was shattered by the knowledge that her prayer had been answered. God had acted—acted with promptitude and with indescribable terror. This was His way, His terrible way, of taking baby to Heaven.

Cook pulled Laura down the front stairs with her.

"Come on now, Miss Laura—don't wait about—we must all get outside the house."

But Nannie and baby could not get outside the house. They were up there, in the nursery, trapped!

Cook plunged heavily down the stairs, pulling Laura after her. But as they passed out through the front door to join Ethel on the lawn, and Cook's grip relaxed, Laura turned back and ran up the stairs again.

Once more she opened the landing door. From somewhere through the smoke she heard a far-off fretful whimpering cry.

And suddenly, something in Laura came alive—warmth, passionate endeavour, that curious incalculable emotion, love.

Her mind was sober and clear. She had read or been told that to rescue people in a fire you dipped a towel in water and put it round your mouth. She ran into her room, soaked the bath towel in the jug, rolled it round her, and crossing the landing plunged into the smoke. There was flame now across the passage, and the timbers were falling. Where an adult would have estimated danger and chances, Laura went bull-headed with the unknowing courage of a child. She *must* get to baby, she must save baby. Otherwise baby would burn to death. She stumbled over the unconscious body of Gwyneth, not knowing what it was. Choking, gasping, she found her way to the crib; the screen round it had protected it from the worst of the smoke.

Laura grabbed at the baby, clutched her close beneath the sheltering wet towel. She stumbled towards the door, her lungs gasping for air.

But there was no retracing her steps. Flames barred her way.

Laura had her wits still. The door to the tank-room—she felt for it, found it, pushed through it to a rickety stair that led up to the tank-room in the loft. She and Charles had got out that way once on to the roof. If she could crawl across the roof . . .

As the fire-engines arrived, an incoherent couple of women in night attire rushed to them crying out:

"The baby—there's a baby and the nurse in that room up there."

The fireman whistled and pursed his lips. That end of the house was blazing with flame. 'Goners,' he said to himself. 'Never get *them* out alive!'

"Everyone else out?" he asked.

Cook, looking round, cried out: "Where's Miss Laura? She came out right after me. Wherever can she be?"

It was then that a fireman called out: "Hi, Joe, there's someone on the roof—the other end. Get a ladder up."

A few moments later, they set their burden down gently on the lawn—an unrecognisable Laura, blackened, her arms scorched, half unconscious, but tight in her grip a small morsel of humanity, whose outraged howls proclaimed her angrily alive.

3

"If it hadn't been for Laura—" Angela stopped, mastering her emotions.

"We've found out all about poor Nannie," she went on.

"It seems she was an epileptic. Her doctor warned her not to take a nurse's post again, but she did. They think she dropped a spirit lamp when she had a fit. I always knew there was something wrong about her—something she didn't want me to find out."

"Poor girl," said Franklin, "she's paid for it."

Angela, ruthless in her mother love, swept on, dismissing the claims of Gwyneth Jones to pity.

"And baby would have been burned to death if it hadn't been for Laura."

"Is Laura all right again?" asked Mr. Baldock.

"Yes. Shock, of course, and her arms were burnt, but not too badly. She'll be quite all right, the doctor says."

"Good for Laura," said Mr. Baldock.

Angela said indignantly: "And you pretending to Arthur that Laura was so jealous of the poor mite that she might do her a mischief! Really—you bachelors!"

"All right, all right," said Mr. Baldock. "I'm not often wrong, but I dare say it's good for me sometimes."

"Just go and take a look at those two."

Mr. Baldock did as he was told. The baby lay on a rug in front of the nursery fire, kicking vaguely and making indeterminate gurgling noises.

Beside her sat Laura. Her arms were bandaged, and she had lost her eyelashes which gave her face a comical appearance. She was dangling some coloured rings to attract the baby's attention. She turned her head to look at Mr. Baldock.

"Hullo, young Laura," said Mr. Baldock. "How are you? Quite the heroine, I hear. A gallant rescue."

Laura gave him a brief glance, and then concentrated once more on her efforts with the rings.

"How are the arms?"

"They did hurt rather a lot, but they've put some stuff on, and they're better now."

"You're a funny one," said Mr. Baldock, sitting down heavily in a chair. "One day you're hoping the cat will smother your baby sister—oh yes, you did—can't deceive me—and the next day you're crawling about the roof lugging the child to safety at the risk of your own life."

"Anyway, I *did* save her," said Laura. "She isn't hurt a bit—not a bit." She bent over the child and spoke passionately. "I won't ever let her be hurt, not ever. I shall look after her all my life."

Mr. Baldock's eyebrows rose slowly.

"So it's love now. You love her, do you?"

"Oh *yes!*" The answer came with the same fervour. "I love her better than anything in the world!"

She turned her face to him, and Mr. Baldock was startled. It was, he thought, like the breaking open of a cocoon. The child's face was radiant with feeling. In spite of the grotesque absence of lashes and brows, the face had a quality of emotion that made it suddenly beautiful.

"I see," said Mr. Baldock. *"I* see . . . And where shall we go from here, I wonder?"

Laura looked at him, puzzled, and slightly apprehensive.

"Isn't it all right?" she asked. "For me to love her, I mean?"

Mr. Baldock looked at her. His face was thoughtful.

"It's all right for *you,* young Laura," he said. "Oh yes, it's all right for you. . . ."

He relapsed into abstraction, his hand tapping his chin.

As a historian he had always mainly been concerned with the past, but there were moments when the fact that he could not foresee the future irritated him profoundly. This was one of them.

He looked at Laura and the crowing Shirley, and his brow contracted angrily. 'Where will they be,' he thought, 'in ten years' time—in twenty years—in twenty-five? Where shall *I* be?'

The answer to that last question came quickly.

'Under the turf,' said Mr. Baldock to himself. 'Under the turf.'

He knew that, but he did not really believe it, any more

than any other positive person full of the vitality of living really believes it.

What a dark and mysterious entity the future was! In twenty-odd years what would have happened? Another war, perhaps? (Most unlikely!) New diseases? People fastening mechanical wings on themselves, perhaps, and floating about the streets like sacrilegious angels! Journeys to Mars? Sustaining oneself on horrid little tablets out of bottles, instead of on steaks and succulent green peas!

"What are you thinking about?" Laura asked.

"The future."

"Do you mean to-morrow?"

"Farther forward than that. I suppose you're able to read, young Laura?"

"Of course," said Laura, shocked. "I've read nearly all the Doctor Dolittles, and the books about Winnie-the-Pooh and—"

"Spare me the horrid details," said Mr. Baldock. "How do you read a book? Begin at the beginning and go right through?"

"Yes. Don't you?"

"No," said Mr. Baldock. "I take a look at the start, get some idea of what it's all about, then I go on to the end and see where the fellow has got to, and what he's been trying to prove. And then, *then* I go back and see *how* he's got there and what's made him land up where he did. Much more interesting."

Laura looked interested but disapproving.

"I don't think that's the way the author meant his book to be read," she said.

"Of course he didn't."

"I think you should read the book the way the author meant."

"Ah," said Mr. Baldock. "But you're forgetting the party of the second part, as the blasted lawyers put it. There's the reader. The reader's got *his* rights, too. The author writes his book the way *he* likes. Has it all his own way. Messes up the punctuation and fools around with the sense any way he pleases. And the reader reads the book the way *he* wants to read it, and the author can't stop him."

"You make it sound like a battle," said Laura.

"I like battles," said Mr. Baldock. "The truth is, we're all slavishly obsessed by Time. Chronological sequence has no significance whatever. If you consider Eternity, you can jump about in Time as you please. But no one does consider Eternity."

Laura had withdrawn her attention from him. She was not considering Eternity. She was considering Shirley.

And watching that dedicated devoted look, Mr. Baldock was again conscious of a vague feeling of apprehension.

part 2

Shirley-1946

Chapter one

1

Shirley walked at a brisk pace along the lane. Her racket with the shoes attached was tucked under one arm. She was smiling to herself and was slightly out of breath.

She must hurry, she would be late for supper. Really, she supposed, she ought not to have played that last set. It hadn't been a good set, anyway. Pam was such a rabbit. Pam and Gordon had been no match at all for Shirley and—what was his name? Henry, anyway. Henry what, she wondered?

Considering Henry, Shirley's feet slowed up a little. Henry was something quite new in her experience. He wasn't in the least like any of the local young men. She considered them impartially. Robin, the vicar's son. Nice, and really very devoted, with rather a pleasant old-world chivalry about him. He was going in for Oriental Languages at the S.O.A.S. and was slightly highbrow. Then there was Peter—Peter was really terribly young and callow. And there was Edward Westbury, who was a good deal older, and worked in a bank, and was rather heavily political. They all belonged here in Bellbury. But Henry came from outside, and had been brought along as somebody's nephew. With Henry had come a sense of liberty and detachment.

Shirley savoured the last word appreciatively. It was a quality she admired.

In Bellbury, there was no detachment, everybody was heavily involved with everybody else.

There was altogether too much family solidarity in Bellbury. Everybody in Bellbury had roots. They belonged.

Shirley was a little confused by these phrases, but they expressed, she thought, what she meant.

Now Henry, definitely, didn't belong. The nearest he would get to it, she thought, was being somebody's nephew, and even then it would probably be an aunt by marriage—not a real aunt.

'Ridiculous, of course,' said Shirley to herself, 'because after all, Henry must have a father and a mother, and a home like everybody else.' But she decided that his parents had probably died in an obscure part of the world, rather young. Or possibly he had a mother who spent all her time on the Riviera, and had had a lot of husbands.

'Ridiculous,' said Shirley again to herself. 'Actually you don't know the first thing about Henry. You don't even know what his surname is—or who brought him this afternoon.'

But it was typical of Henry, she felt, that she should not know. Henry, she thought, would always appear like that—vague, with an insubstantial background—and then he would depart again, and still nobody would know what his name was, or whose nephew he had been. He was just at attractive young man, with an engaging smile, who played tennis extremely well.

Shirley liked the cool way in which, when Mary Crofton had pondered: "Now how had we better play?" Henry had immediately said:

"I'll play with Shirley against you two," and had thereupon spun a racket saying: "Rough or smooth?"

Henry, she was quite sure, would always do exactly as he pleased.

She had asked him: "Are you down here for long?"

and he had replied vaguely: "Oh, I shouldn't think so."

He hadn't suggested their meeting again.

A momentary frown passed over Shirley's face. She wished he had done so. . . .

Again she glanced at her watch, and quickened her steps. She was really going to be very late. Not that Laura would mind. Laura never minded. Laura was an angel. . . .

The house was in sight now. Mellow in its early Georgian beauty, it had a slightly lop-sided effect, due, so she understood, to a fire which had consumed one wing of it, which had never been rebuilt.

Irresistibly Shirley's pace slackened. Somehow to-day, she didn't want to get home. She didn't want to go inside those kindly enclosing walls, the late sun streaming in through the west windows on to the gentle faded chintzes. The stillness there was so peaceful; there would be Laura with her warm welcoming face, her watchful protecting eyes, and Ethel stumping in with the supper dishes. Warmth, love, protection, home. . . . All the things, surely, most valuable in life? And they were hers, without effort or desire on her part, surrounding her, pressing on her. . . .

'Now that's a curious way of putting it,' thought Shirley to herself. 'Pressing on me? What on earth do I mean by that?'

But it was, exactly, what she was feeling. Pressure—definite, steady pressure. Like the weight of the knapsack she had carried once on a walking tour. Almost unnoticed at first, and then steadily making itself felt, bearing down, cutting into her shoulders, weighing down on her. A burden. . . .

'Really, the things I think of!' said Shirley to herself, and running up to the open front door, she went in.

The hall was in semi-twilight. From the floor above, Laura called down the well of the staircase in her soft, rather husky voice:

"Is that you, Shirley?"

"Yes, I'm afraid I'm frightfully late, Laura."

"It doesn't matter at all. It's only macaroni—the *au gratin* kind. Ethel has got it in the oven."

Laura Franklin came round the bend of the staircase, a slim fragile creature, with an almost colourless face and deep brown eyes set at an unusual angle that made them, in some curious way, look tragic.

She came down, smiling at Shirley.

"Enjoy yourself?"

"Oh yes," said Shirley.

"Good tennis?"

"Not bad."

"Anybody exciting? Or just Bellbury?"

"Mostly Bellbury."

Funny how when people asked you questions, you didn't want to answer them. And yet the answers were so harmless. Naturally Laura liked to know how she'd enjoyed herself.

If people were fond of you, they always wanted to know—

Would Henry's people want to know? She tried to visualize Henry at home, but failed. It sounded ridiculous, but she couldn't somehow *see* Henry in a home. And yet he must have one!

A nebulous picture swam before her eyes. Henry strolling into a room where his mother, a platinum blonde just back from the South of France, was carefully painting her mouth a rather surprising colour. "Hullo, Mother, so you're back?"—"Yes, have you been playing tennis?"—"Yes." There would be no curiosity, practically no interest. Henry and his mother would both be quite indifferent to what the other had been doing.

Laura asked curiously:

"What are you saying to yourself, Shirley? Your lips are moving, and your eyebrows are going up and down."

Shirley laughed:

"Oh, just an imaginary conversation."

Laura raised delicate eyebrows.

"It seemed to please you."

"It was quite ridiculous really."

The faithful Ethel put her head round the dining-room door and said:

"Supper's in."

Shirley cried: "I must wash," and ran upstairs.

After supper, as they sat in the drawing-room, Laura said: "I got the prospectus from the St. Katherine's Secretarial College to-day. I gather it's one of the best of its kind. What do you feel about it, Shirley?"

A grimace marred the loveliness of Shirley's young face.

"Learn shorthand and typing and then go and take a job?"

"Why not?"

Shirley sighed, and then laughed.

"Because I'm a lazy devil. I'd much rather stay at home and do nothing. Laura darling, I've been at school for *years!* Can't I have a bit of a break?"

"I wish there was something you really wished to train for, or were keen about." A frown showed itself for a moment on Laura's forehead.

"I'm a throw-back," said Shirley. "I just want to sit at home and dream of a big handsome husband, and plenty of family allowances for a growing family."

Laura did not respond. She was still looking worried.

"If you do a course at St. Katherine's, it's a question, really, of where you should live in London. Would you like to be a P.G.—with Cousin Angela, perhaps—"

"*Not* Cousin Angela. Have a heart, Laura."

"Not Angela then, but with some family or other. Or there are hostels, I believe. Later, you could share a flat with another girl."

"Why can't I share a flat with you?" demanded Shirley.

Laura shook her head.

"I'd stay here."

"Stay here? Not come to London with me?"

Shirley sounded indignant and incredulous.

Laura said simply: "I don't want to be bad for you, darling."

"Bad for me? How could you be?"

"Well—possessive, you know."

"Like the kind of mother who eats her young? Laura, you're never possessive."

Laura said dubiously: "I hope I'm not, but one never knows." She added with a frown: "One doesn't know in the least what one is really like. . . ."

"Well, I really don't think you need have qualms, Laura. You're not in the least the domineering kind—at least not to me. You don't boss or bully, or try to arrange my life for me."

"Well, actually, that is exactly what I am doing—arranging for you to take a secretarial course in London when you don't in the least want to!"

The sisters both laughed.

2

Laura straightened her back and stretched her arms.

"Four dozen," she said.

She had been bunching sweet-peas.

"We ought to get a good price from Trendle's," she said. "Long stalks, and four flowers on each stem. The sweet-peas have been a success this year, Horder."

Horder, who was a gnarled, dirty, and gloomy-looking old man growled a qualified assent.

"Not too bad this year, they ain't," he said grudgingly.

Horder was a man very sure of his position. An elderly, retired gardener, who really knew his trade, his price at the end of five years of war was above rubies. Everyone had competed for him. Laura by sheer force of personality had got him, though Mrs. Kindle, whose husband was rumoured to have made a fortune out of munitions, had offered him much more money.

But Horder had preferred to work for Miss Franklin. Known her father and mother, he had; proper folk, gen-

tlefolk. He remembered Miss Laura as a little bit of a
thing. These sentiments alone would not have retained
his services. The truth was that he liked working for Miss
Laura. Proper drove you, she did, not much chance for
slackness. If she'd been out, she knew just how much you
ought to have got on with. But then, too, she appreciated
what you'd done. She was free with her praise and her
admiration. Generous, too, in elevenses and frequent
cups of hot, strong, sugary tea. Wasn't everyone who was
free with their tea and sugar nowadays, seeing it was ra-
tioned. And she was a fine quick worker herself, Miss
Laura was, she could bunch quicker than he could—and
that was saying something. And she'd got ideas—always
looking towards the future—planning this and that—
going in for new-fangled notions. Them cloches, for instance. Horder had taken a poor view of cloches. Laura
admitted to him that of course she might be wrong. . . .
On this basis, Horder graciously consented to give the
new-fangled things a trial. The tomatoes had achieved results that surprised him.

"Five o'clock," said Laura, glancing at her watch.
"We've got through very well."

She looked round her, at the metal vases and cans filled
with to-morrow's quota, to be taken into Milchester,
where she supplied a florist and a greengrocer.

"Wonderful price vedges fetch," old Horder remarked
appreciatively. "Never wouldn't have believed it."

"All the same, I'm sure we're right to start switching
over to cut flowers. People have been starved for them all
through the war, and everybody's growing vegetables
now."

"Ah!" said Horder, "things aren't what they used to be.
In your pa and ma's time, growing things for the market
wouldn't have been thought of. I mind this place as it
used to be—a picture! Mr. Webster was in charge, he
came just before the fire, he did. That fire! Lucky the
whole house didn't burn down."

Laura nodded, and slipped off the rubber apron she

had been wearing. Horder's words had taken her mind back many years. *"Just before the fire—"*

The fire had been a kind of turning-point in her life. She saw herself dimly before it—an unhappy jealous child, longing for attention, for love.

But on the night of the fire, a new Laura had come into existence—a Laura whose life had become suddenly and satisfyingly full. From the moment that she had struggled through smoke and flames with Shirley in her arms, her life had found its object and meaning—to care for Shirley.

She had saved Shirley from death. Shirley was hers. All in a moment (so it seemed to her now) those two important figures, her father and mother, had receded into the middle distance. Her eager longing for their notice, for their need of her, had diminished and faded. Perhaps she had not so much loved them as craved for *them* to love *her*. Love was what she had felt so suddenly for that small entity of flesh named Shirley. Satisfying all cravings, fulfilling her vaguely-understood need. It was no longer she, Laura, who mattered—it was Shirley. . . .

She would look after Shirley, see that no harm came to her, watch out for predatory cats, wake up at night and be sure that there was no second fire; fetch and carry for Shirley, bring her toys, play games with her when she was older, nurse her if she were ill. . . .

The child of eleven couldn't, of course, foresee the future: the Franklins, taking a brief holiday together, flying to Le Touquet and the plane crashing on the return journey. . . .

Laura had been fourteen then, and Shirley three. There had been no near relatives; old Cousin Angela had been the nearest. It was Laura who had made her plans, weighing them carefully, trimming them to meet with approval, and then submitting them with all the force of indomitable decision. An elderly lawyer and Mr. Baldock had been the executors and trustees. Laura proposed that she should leave school and live at home, an excellent nanny would continue to look after Shirley. Miss Weekes should give up her cottage and come to live in the house, educating Laura, and being normally in charge of the household. It was an excellent suggestion, practical and easy to carry out, only feebly opposed by Mr. Baldock on the grounds that he disliked Girton women, and that Miss Weekes would get ideas in her head, and turn Laura into a blue-stocking.

But Laura had no doubts about Miss Weekes—it would not be Miss Weekes who would run things. Miss Weekes was a woman of intellect, with an enthusiasm that ran to passion for mathematics. Domestic administration would not interest her. The plan had worked well. Laura was splendidly educated, Miss Weekes had an ease of living formerly denied to her, Laura saw to it that no clashes occurred between Mr. Baldock and Miss Weekes. The choice of new servants if needed, the decision for Shirley to attend, first a kindergarten school, later a convent in a near-by town, though apparently all originated by Miss Weekes, were in reality Laura's suggestions. The household was a harmonious one. Later Shirley was sent to a famous boarding-school. Laura was then twenty-two.

A year after that, the war broke out, and altered the pattern of existence. Shirley's school was transferred to new premises in Wales. Miss Weekes went to London and obtained a post in a Ministry. The house was requisitioned by the Air Ministry to house officers; Laura transferred herself to the gardener's cottage, and worked as a land-girl on an adjacent farm, managing at the same time to cultivate vegetables in her own big walled garden.

And now, a year ago, the war with Germany had ended. The house had been de-requisitioned with startling abruptness. Laura had to attempt the re-establishment of it as something faintly like a home. Shirley had come home from school for good, declining emphatically to continue her studies by going to a university.

She was not, she said, the brainy kind! Her headmistress in a letter to Laura confirmed this statement in slightly different terms:

"I really do not feel that Shirley is the type to benefit by a university education. She is a dear girl, and very intelligent, but definitely not the academic type."

So Shirley had come home, and that old stand-by, Ethel, who had been working in a factory which was now abandoning war work, gave up her job and arrived back, not as the correct house-parlourmaid she had once been, but as a general factotum and friend. Laura continued and elaborated her plans for vegetable and flower production. Incomes were not what they had been with present taxation. If she and Shirley were to keep their home, the garden must be made to pay for itself and, it was to be hoped, show a profit.

That was the picture of the past that Laura saw in her mind, as she unfastened her apron and went into the house to wash. All through the years, the central figure of the pattern had been Shirley.

A baby Shirley, staggering about, telling Laura in stuttering unintelligible language what her dolls were doing. An older Shirley, coming back from kindergarten, pouring out confused descriptions of Miss Duckworth, of Tommy this and Mary that, of the naughty things Robin had done, and what Peter had drawn in his reading-book, and what Miss Duck had said about it.

An older Shirley had come back from boarding-school, brimming over with information: the girls she liked, the girls she hated, the angelic disposition of Miss Geoffrey, the English mistress, the despicable meannesses of Miss Andrews, the mathematics mistress, the indignities practised by all on the French mistress. Shirley had always chatted easily and unself-consciously to Laura. Their relationship was in a way a curious one—not quite that of sisters, since the gap in years separated them, yet not removed by a generation, as a parent and child would be. There had never been any need for Laura to ask questions. Shirley would be bubbling over—"Oh, Laura, I've got such lots to tell you!" And Laura would listen, laugh, comment, disagree, approve, as the case might be.

Now that Shirley had come home for good, it had seemed to Laura that everything was exactly the same. Every day saw an interchange of comment on any separate activities they had pursued. Shirley talked unconcernedly of Robin Grant, of Edward Westbury; she had a frank affectionate nature, and it was natural to her, or so it had seemed, to comment daily on what happened.

But yesterday she had come back from tennis at the Hargreaves and had been oddly monosyllabic in her replies to Laura's questions.

Laura wondered why. Of course, Shirley was growing up. She would have her own thoughts, her own life. That was only natural and right. What Laura had to decide was how best that could be accomplished. Laura sighed, looked at her watch again, and decided to go and see Mr. Baldock.

Chapter two

1

Mr. Baldock was busy in his garden when Laura came up the path. He grunted and immediately asked:

"What do you think of my begonias? Pretty good?"

Mr. Baldock was actually an exceedingly poor gardener, but was inordinately proud of the results he achieved and completely oblivious of any failures. It was expected of his friends not to refer to these latter. Laura gazed obediently on some rather sparse begonias and said they were very nice.

"Nice? They're magnificent!" Mr. Baldock, who was now an old man and considerably stouter than he had been eighteen years ago, groaned a little as he bent over once more to pull at some weeds.

"It's this wet summer," he grumbled. "Fast as you clear the beds, up the stuff comes again. Words fail me when it comes to what I think of bindweed! You may say what you like, but *I* think it is directly inspired by the devil!" He puffed a little, then said, his words coming shortly between stertorous breaths: "Well, young Laura, what is it? Trouble? Tell me about it."

"I always come to you when I'm worried. I have ever since I was six."

"Rum little kid you were. Peaky face and great big eyes."

"I wish I knew whether I was doing right."

"Shouldn't bother if I was you," said Mr. Baldock. "Garrrrr! Get up, you unspeakable brute!" (This was to the bindweed.) "No, as I say, I shouldn't bother. Some people know what's right and wrong, and some people haven't the least idea. It's like an ear for music!"

"I don't think I really meant right or wrong in the moral sense, I think I meant was I being wise?"

"Well, that's quite a different thing. On the whole, one does far more foolish things than wise ones. What's the problem?"

"It's Shirley."

"Naturally it's Shirley. You never think of anything or anyone else."

"I've been arranging for her to go to London and train in secretarial work."

"Seems to me remarkably silly," said Mr. Baldock. "Shirley is a nice child, but the last person in the world to make a competent secretary."

"Still, she's got to do something."

"So they say nowadays."

"And I'd like her to meet people."

"Blast and curse and damn that nettle," said Mr. Baldock, shaking an injured hand. "People? What d'you mean by *people?* Crowds? Employers? Other girls? Young men?"

"I suppose really I mean young men."

Mr. Baldock chuckled.

"She's not doing too badly down here. That mother's boy, Robin, at the vicarage seems to be making sheep's eyes at her, young Peter has got it badly, and even Edward Westbury has started putting brilliantine on what's left of his hair. Smelt it in church last Sunday. Thought to myself: 'Now, who's *he* after?' And sure enough there he was when we came out, wriggling like an embarrassed dog as he talked to her."

"I don't think she cares about any of them."

"Why should she? Give her time. She's very young,

Laura. Come now, why do you really want to send her away to London, or are you going too?"

"Oh no. That's the whole point."

Mr. Baldock straightened up.

"So that's the point, is it?" He eyed her curiously. "What exactly is in your mind, Laura?"

Laura looked down at the gravel path.

"As you said just now, Shirley is the only thing that matters to me. I—I love her so much that I'm afraid of— well, of hurting her. Of trying to tie her to me too closely."

Mr. Baldock's voice was unexpectedly gentle.

"She's ten years younger than you are, and in some ways she's more like a daughter than a sister to you."

"I've mothered her, yes."

He nodded.

"And you realise, being intelligent, that maternal love is a possessive love?"

"Yes, that's exactly it. And I don't want it to be like that. I want Shirley to be free and—well—free."

"And that's at the bottom of pushing her out of the nest? Sending her out in the world to find her feet?"

"Yes. But what I'm so uncertain about is—am I wise to do so?"

Mr. Baldock rubbed his nose in an irritable way.

"You women!" he said. "Trouble with all of you is, you make such a song and dance about things. How is one ever to know what's wise or not? If young Shirley goes to London and picks up with an Egyptian student and has a coffee-coloured baby in Bloomsbury, you'll say it's all your fault, whereas it will be entirely Shirley's and possibly the Egyptian's. And if she trains and gets a good job as a secretary and marries her boss, then you'll say you were justified. All bunkum! You *can't* arrange other people's lives for them. Either Shirley's got some sense or she hasn't. Time will show. If you think this London idea is a good plan, go ahead with it, but don't take it so seriously. That's the whole trouble with you, Laura, you take life seriously. It's the trouble with a lot of women."

"And you don't?"

"I take bindweed seriously," said Mr. Baldock, glaring down balefully at the heap on the path. *"And* greenfly. And I take my stomach seriously, because it gives me hell if I don't. But I never dream of taking other people's lives seriously. I've too much respect for them, for one thing."

"You don't understand. I couldn't bear it if Shirley made a mess of her life and was unhappy."

"Fiddle de dee," said Mr. Baldock rudely. "What does it matter if Shirley's unhappy? Most people are, off and on. You've got to stick being unhappy in this life, just as you've got to stick everything else. You need courage to get through this world, courage and a gay heart."

He looked at her sharply.

"What about yourself, Laura?"

"Myself?" said Laura, surprised.

"Yes. Suppose *you're* unhappy? Are you going to be able to bear that?"

Laura smiled.

"I've never thought about it."

"Well, why not? Think about yourself a bit more. Unselfishness in a woman can be as disastrous as a heavy hand in pastry. What do *you* want out of life? You're twenty-eight, a good marriageable age. Why don't you do a bit of man-hunting?"

"How absurd you are, Baldy."

"Thistles and ground elder!" roared Mr. Baldock. "You're a woman, aren't you? A not bad-looking, perfectly normal woman. Or aren't you normal? What's your reaction when a man tries to kiss you?"

"They haven't very often tried," said Laura.

"And why the hell not? Because you're not doing your stuff." He shook a finger at her. "You're thinking the whole time of something else. There you stand in a nice neat coat and skirt looking the nice modest sort of girl my mother would have approved of. Why don't you paint your lips pillar-box red and varnish your nails to match?"

Laura stared at him.

"You've always said you hated lipstick and red nails."

"Hate them? Of course *I* hate them. I'm seventy-nine! But they're a symbol, a sign that you're in the market and ready to play at Nature's game. A kind of mating call, that's what they are. Now look here, Laura, you're not everybody's fancy. You don't flaunt a banner of sex, looking as though you weren't able to help it, as some women do. There's one particular kind of man who might come and hunt you out without your doing anything about it—the kind of man that has the sense to know that you're the woman for him. But it's long odds against that happening. You've got to do your bit. You've got to remember that you're a woman, and play the part of a woman and look about for your man."

"Darling Baldy, I love your lectures, but I've always been hopelessly plain."

"So you *want* to be an old maid?"

Laura flushed a little.

"No, of course I don't. I just don't think it's likely that I shall marry."

"Defeatism!" roared Mr. Baldock.

"No, indeed it isn't. I just think it's impossible that anyone should fall in love with me."

"Men can fall in love with anything," said Mr. Baldock rudely. "With hare lips, and acne, and prognathous jaws and with numb-skulls and cretins! Just think of half the married women you know! No, young Laura, you just don't want to bother! You want to love—not to be loved —and I dare say you've got something there. To be loved is to carry a heavy burden."

"You think I do love Shirley too much? That I am possessive?"

"No," said Mr. Baldock slowly, "I don't think you are possessive. I acquit you of *that*."

"Then—can one love anyone too much?"

"Of course one can!" he roared. "One can do anything

too much. Eat too much, drink too much, love too much . . ."

He quoted:

> *"I've known a thousand ways of love*
> *And each one made the loved one rue."*

"Put that in your pipe, young Laura, and smoke it."

2

Laura walked home, smiling to herself. As she entered the house, Ethel appeared from the back premises, and spoke in a confidential whisper:

"There's a gentleman waiting for you—a Mr. Glyn-Edwards, quite a young gentleman. I put him in the drawing-room. Said he'd wait. He's all right— not vacuums I mean, or hard luck stories."

Laura smiled a little, but she trusted Ethel's judgment.

Glyn-Edwards? She could not recall the name. Perhaps it was one of the young flying officers who had been billeted here during the war.

She went across the hall and into the drawing-room.

The young man who rose quickly as she came in was a complete stranger to her.

That, indeed, in the years to come, was to remain her feeling about Henry. He was a stranger. Never for one moment did he become anything else.

The young man was smiling, an eager, rather charming smile which suddenly wavered. He seemed taken aback.

"Miss Franklin?" he said. "But you're not—" His smile suddenly widened again, confidently. "I expect she's your sister."

"You mean Shirley?"

"That's it," said Henry, with evident relief. "Shirley. I met her yesterday— at a tennis-party. My name's Henry Glyn-Edwards."

"Do sit down," said Laura. "Shirley ought to be back

soon. She went to tea at the vicarage. Won't you have some sherry? Or would you rather have gin?"

Henry said he would prefer sherry.

They sat there talking. Henry's manner was just right, it had that touch of diffidence that is disarming. A charm of manner that was too assured might have aroused antagonism. As it was, he talked easily and gaily, without awkwardness, but deferring to Laura in a pleasant well-bred manner.

"Are you staying in Bellbury?" Laura asked.

"Oh no. I'm staying with my aunt over at Endsmoor."

Endsmoor was well over sixty miles away, the other side of Milchester. Laura felt a little surprised. Henry seemed to see that a certain amount of explanation was required.

"I went off with someone else's tennis-racket yesterday," he said. "Awfully stupid of me. So I thought I'd run over to return it and find my own. I managed to wangle some petrol."

He looked at her blandly.

"Did you find your racket all right?"

"Oh yes," said Henry. "Lucky, wasn't it? I'm afraid I'm awfully vague about things. Over in France, you know, I was always losing my kit."

He blinked disarmingly.

"So as I *was* over here," he said, "I thought I'd look up Shirley."

Was there, or was there not, some faint sign of embarrassment?

If there was, Laura liked him none the worse for it. Indeed, she preferred that to too much assurance.

This young man was likeable, eminently so. She felt the charm he exuded quite distinctly. What she could not account for was her own definite feeling of hostility.

Possessiveness again, Laura wondered? If Shirley had met Henry the day before, it seemed odd that she should not have mentioned him.

They continued to talk. It was now past seven. Henry

was clearly not bound by conventional hours of calling. He was obviously remaining here until he saw Shirley. Laura wondered how much longer Shirley was going to be. She was usually home before this.

Murmuring an excuse to Henry, Laura left the room and went into the study where the telephone was. She rang up the vicarage.

The vicar's wife answered.

"Shirley? Oh yes, Laura, she's here. She's playing clock golf with Robin. I'll get her."

There was a pause, and then Shirley's voice, gay, alive. "Laura?"

Laura said dryly:

"You've got a follower."

"A follower? Who?"

"His name's Glyn-Edwards. He blew in an hour and a half ago, and he's still here. I don't think he means to leave without seeing you. Both his conversation and mine are wearing rather thin!"

"Glyn-Edwards? I've never heard of him. Oh dear—I suppose I'd better come home and cope. Pity. I'm well on the way to beating Robin's record."

"He was at the tennis yesterday, I gather."

"Not *Henry?*"

Shirley's voice sounded breathless, slightly incredulous. The note in it surprised Laura.

"It could be Henry," she said dryly. "He's staying with an aunt over at—"

Shirley, breathless, interrupted:

"It *is* Henry. I'll come at once."

Laura put down the receiver with a slight sense of shock. She went back slowly into the drawing-room.

"Shirley will be back soon," she said, and added that she hoped Henry would stay to supper.

3

Laura leaned back in her chair at the head of the dinner-table and watched the other two. It was still only dusk, not dark, and the windows were uncurtained. The evening light was kind to the two young faces that bent towards each other so easily.

Watching them dispassionately, Laura tried to understand her own mounting feeling of uneasiness. Was it simply that she had taken a dislike to Henry? No, it could hardly be that. She acknowledged Henry's charm, his likeability, his good manners. Since, as yet, she knew nothing about him, she could hardly form a considered judgment. He was perhaps a little too casual, too off-hand, too detached? Yes, that explained it best—detached.

Surely the core of her feeling was rooted in Shirley. She was experiencing the sharp sense of shock which comes when you discover an unknown facet in someone about whom you are assured you know everything. Laura and Shirley were not unduly demonstrative to each other, but stretching back over the years was the figure of Shirley, pouring out to Laura her hates, her loves, her desires, her frustrations.

But yesterday, when Laura had asked casually: "Anybody exciting? Or just Bellbury?" Shirley had replied nonchalantly: "Oh, mostly Bellbury."

Laura wondered why Shirley hadn't mentioned Henry. She remembered the sudden breathlessness just now in Shirley's voice as she had said, over the telephone *"Henry?"*

Her mind came back to the conversation going on so close to her.

Henry was just concluding a sentence. . . .

"—if you liked. I'd pick you up in Carswell."

"Oh, I'd love it. I've never been much to race meetings. . . ."

"Marldon's a tin-pot one, but a friend of mine's got a horse running. We might . . ."

Laura reflected calmly and dispassionately that this was a courtship. Henry's unexplained appearance, the wangled petrol, the inadequate excuse—he was sharply attracted by Shirley. She did not tell herself that this all might come to nothing. She believed, on the contrary, that she saw events casting their shadows before them.

Henry and Shirley would marry. She knew it, she was sure of it. And Henry was a stranger. . . . She would never really know Henry any better than she knew him now.

Would Shirley ever know him?

Chapter three

1

"I wonder," said Henry, "if you ought to come and meet my aunt."

He looked at Shirley doubtfully.

"I'm afraid," he said, "that it will be an awful bore for you."

They were leaning over the rail of the paddock, gazing unseeingly at the only horse, Number Nineteen, which was being led monotonously round and round.

This was the third race meeting Shirley had attended in Henry's company. Where other young men's ideas ran to the pictures, Henry's seemed to be concerned with sport. It was all on a par with the exciting difference between Henry and other young men.

"I'm sure I shouldn't be bored," said Shirley politely.

"I don't really see how you could help it," said Henry. "She does horoscopes and has queer ideas about the Pyramids."

"Do you know, Henry, I don't even know what your aunt's name is?"

"Don't you?" said Henry, surprised.

"Is it Glyn-Edwards?"

"No. It's Fairborough. Lady Muriel Fairborough. She's not bad really. Doesn't mind how you come and go. And always very decent at stumping up in a crisis."

"That's a very depressed-looking horse," said Shirley, looking at Number Nineteen. She was nerving herself to say something quite different.

"Wretched brute," agreed Henry. "One of Tommy Twisdon's worst. Come down over the first hurdle, I should think."

Two more horses were brought into the ring, and more people arrived to lean over the rails.

"What's this? Third race?" Henry consulted his card. "Are the numbers up yet? Is Number Eighteen running?"

Shirley glanced up at the board behind her.

"Yes."

"We might have a bit on that, if the price is all right."

"You know a lot about horses, don't you, Henry? Were you—were you brought up with horses?"

"My experience has mostly been with bookmakers."

Shirley nerved herself to ask what she had been wanting to ask.

"It's funny, isn't it, how little I really know about you? Have you got a father or mother, or are you an orphan, like me?"

"Oh! My father and mother were killed in the Blitz. They were in the Café de Paris."

"Oh! Henry—how awful!"

"Yes, wasn't it?" agreed Henry, without, however, displaying undue emotion. He seemed to feel this himself, for he added: "Of course it's over four years ago now. I was quite fond of them and all that, but one can't go on remembering things, can one?"

"I suppose not," said Shirley doubtfully.

"Why all this thirst for information?" asked Henry.

"Well—one likes to know about people," Shirley spoke almost apologetically.

"Does one?" Henry seemed genuinely surprised.

"Anyway," he decided, "you'd better come and meet my aunt. Put it all on a proper footing with Laura."

"Laura?"

"Well, Laura's the conventional type, isn't she? Satisfy

her that I'm respectable and all that."

And very shortly afterwards, a polite note arrived from Lady Muriel, inviting Shirley to lunch, and saying Henry would call for her in the car.

2

Henry's aunt bore a strong resemblance to the White Queen. Her costume was a jumble of different and brightly-coloured wool garments, she knitted assiduously, and she had a bun of faded brown hair, streaked with grey, from which untidy wisps descended in all directions.

She managed to combine the qualities of briskness and vagueness.

"So nice you could come, my dear," she said warmly, shaking Shirley by the hand and dropping a ball of wool. "Pick it up, Henry, there's a good boy. Now tell me, when were you born?"

Shirley said that she was born on September 18th, 1928.

"Ah yes. Virgo—I thought so. And the time?"

"I'm afraid I don't know."

"Tck! How annoying! You must find out and let me know. It's most important. Where are my other needles— the number eights? I'm knitting for the Navy—a pullover with a high neck."

She held out the garment.

"It will have to be for a very large sailor," said Henry.

"Well, I expect they have all sizes in the Navy," said Lady Muriel comfortably. "And in the Army, too," she added inconsequently. "I remember Major Tug Murray —sixteen stone—special polo ponies to be up to his weight—and when he rode anyone off there was nothing they could do about it. Broke his neck when he was out with the Pytchley," she added cheerfully.

A very old and shaky butler opened the door and announced that luncheon was served.

They went into the dining-room. The meal was an indifferent one, and the table silver was tarnished.

"Poor old Melsham," said Lady Muriel when the butler was out of the room. "He really can't see *at all*. And he shakes so when he hands things, that I'm never sure if he'll get round the table safely. I've told him again and again to put things on the sideboard, but he won't. And he won't let any of the silver be put away, though of course he can't see to clean it. And he quarrels with all the queer girls which are all one gets nowadays—not what he's been accustomed to, he says. Well, I mean, what is? With the war and all."

They returned to the drawing-room, and Lady Muriel conducted a brisk conversation on biblical prophecies, the measurements of the Pyramids, how much one should pay for illicit clothing coupons, and the difficulties of herbaceous borders.

After which she rolled up her knitting with great suddenness, and announced that she was going to take Shirley round the garden and dispatched Henry with a message to the chauffeur.

"He's a dear boy, Henry," she said as she and Shirley set forth. "Very selfish, of course, and frightfully extravagant. But what can you expect—brought up as he has been?"

"Does he—take after his mother?" Shirley felt her way cautiously.

"Oh dear me, no. Poor Mildred was always most economical. It was quite a passion with her. I can't think why my brother ever married her—she wasn't even a pretty girl, and deadly dull. I believe she was very happy when they were out on a farm in Kenya among the serious farming kind. Later, of course, they got into the gay set, which didn't suit her nearly as well."

"Henry's father—" Shirley paused.

"Poor dear Ned. He went through the Bankruptcy Court three times. But such good company. Henry reminds me of him sometimes. That's a very special kind of

alstroemeria—it doesn't do everywhere. I've had a lot of
success with it."

She tweaked off a dead bloom and glanced sideways
at Shirley.

"How pretty you are, my dear—you mustn't mind my
saying so. And very young, too."

"I'm nearly nineteen."

"Yes . . . I see . . . Do you do things—like all
these clever girls nowadays?"

"I'm not clever," said Shirley. "My sister wants me to
take a secretarial course."

"I'm sure that would be very nice. Secretary to an M.P.
perhaps. Everyone says that's *so* interesting; I've never
seen why. But I don't suppose you'll do anything long—
you'll get married."

She sighed.

"Such an odd world nowadays. I've just had a letter
from one of my oldest friends. Her girl has just married
a dentist. A *dentist*. In my young days, girls didn't marry
dentists. Doctors, yes, but not dentists."

She turned her head.

"Ah, here comes Henry. Well, Henry, I suppose you're
going to take Miss—Miss—"

"Franklin."

"Miss Franklin away from me."

"I thought we'd run over to Bury Heath."

"Have you been getting petrol out of Harman?"

"Just a couple of gallons, Aunt Muriel."

"Well, I won't have it, do you hear? You must wangle
your own petrol. I have trouble enough getting mine."

"You don't really mind, darling. Come now."

"Well—just this once. Good-bye, my dear. Now mind
you send me those particulars about time of birth—don't
forget—then I can get your horoscope worked out properly. You should wear green, dear—all Virgo people
should wear green."

"I'm Aquarius," said Henry. "January 20th."

"Unstable," snapped his aunt, "remember that, my

dear. All Aquariuses—most undependable."

"I hope you weren't too bored," said Henry as they drove away.

"I wasn't bored at all. I think your aunt's sweet."

"Oh, I wouldn't go as far as that. But she's not too bad."

"She's very fond of you."

"Oh, not really. She doesn't mind having me about."

He added: "My leave's nearly over. I ought to be de-mobbed soon."

"What are you going to do then?"

"I don't really know. I thought of the Bar."

"Yes?"

"But that's rather a sweat. I think perhaps I might go into a business of some kind."

"What kind?"

"Well, it rather depends where one has a pal to give one a start. I've got one or two banking connections. And I know a couple of tycoons who'd graciously allow me to start at the bottom." He added: "I've not got much money, you know. Three hundred a year to be exact. Of my own, I mean. Most of my relations are as mean as hell—no good for a touch. Good old Muriel comes to the rescue now and again, but she's a bit straitened herself nowadays. I've got a godmother who's reasonably generous if one puts it to her the right way. It's all a bit unsatisfactory, I know. . . ."

"Why," said Shirley, puzzled by this sudden flood of information, "are you telling me all this?"

Henry blushed. The car wobbled in a drunken manner. He spoke in an indistinct mumble.

"Thought you knew . . . Darling—you're so lovely . . . I want to marry you . . . You must marry me—you *must*—you *must*. . . ."

3

Laura looked at Henry with a kind of desperation.

It was exactly, she thought, like climbing up a steep hill on an icy day—you slipped back as fast as you advanced.

"Shirley is too young," she said, "far too young."

"Come now, Laura, she's nineteen. One of my grand-mothers was married at sixteen, and had twins before she was eighteen."

"That was a long time ago."

"And lots of people have married young in the war."

"And have already lived to regret it."

"Don't you think you're taking rather a gloomy view? Shirley and I shan't regret."

"You don't know that."

"Oh, but I do," he grinned at her. "I'm positive. I do really love Shirley madly. And I shall do everything I can to make her happy."

He looked at her hopefully. He said again:

"I really do love her."

As before, his patent sincerity disarmed Laura. He did love Shirley.

"I know, of course, that I'm not particularly well off—"

There again he was disarming. For it wasn't the fi-nancial angle that worried Laura. She had no ambition for Shirley to make what is called a 'good match.' Henry and Shirley would not have a large income to start life on. but they would have enough, if they were careful. Henry's prospects were no worse than those of hundreds of other young men released from the services with their way to make. He had good health, good brains, great charm of manner. Yes, perhaps that was it. It was his charm that made Laura mistrust him. No one had any right to have as much charm as Henry had.

She spoke again, a tone of authority in her voice.

"No, Henry. There can be no question of marriage as yet. A year's engagement, at least. That gives you both time to be sure you know your own minds."

"Really, Laura dear, you might be at least fifty. A

heavy Victorian father rather than a sister."

"I have to stand in the place of a father to Shirley. That gives time for you to find a job and get yourself established."

"How depressing it all sounds." His smile was still charming. "I don't believe you want Shirley to marry *anybody*."

Laura flushed.

"Nonsense."

Henry was pleased with the success of his stray shaft. He went away to find Shirley.

"Laura," he said, "is being tiresome. Why shouldn't we get married? I don't want to wait. I hate waiting for things. Don't you? If one waits too long for anything, one loses interest. Of course we could go off and get quietly married at a registry office somewhere. How about it? It would save a lot of fuss."

"Oh no, Henry, we couldn't do *that*."

"I don't see why not? As I say, it would save a lot of fuss all round."

"I'm under age. Wouldn't we have to have Laura's consent?"

"Yes, I suppose you would. She's your legal guardian, isn't she? Or is it old what's his name?"

"I don't believe I actually know. Baldy is my trustee."

"The trouble is," said Henry, "that Laura doesn't like me."

"Oh, she does, Henry. I'm sure she does."

"No, she doesn't. She's jealous, of course."

Shirley looked troubled.

"Do you really think so?"

"She never *has* liked me—from the beginning. And I've taken a lot of trouble to be nice to her." Henry sounded injured.

"I know. You're sweet to her. But after all, Henry, we have sprung this rather suddenly on her. We've only known each other—what?—three weeks. I suppose it doesn't *really* matter if we have to wait a year."

"Darling, *I* don't want to wait a year. I want to marry you now—next week—to-morrow. Don't you want to marry me?"

"Oh, Henry, I do—I do."

4

Mr. Baldock had duly been asked to dinner to meet Henry. Afterwards Laura had demanded breathlessly:

"Well, what do you think of him?"

"Now, now, slowly. How can I judge across a dinner-table? Nice manners, doesn't treat me as an old fogey. Listens to me deferentially."

"Is that all you've got to say? Is he good enough for Shirley?"

"Nobody, my dear Laura, will ever be good enough for Shirley in your eyes."

"No, perhaps that's true . . . But do you like him?"

"Yes, I like him. What I'd call an agreeable fellow."

"You think he'll make her a good husband."

"Oh, I wouldn't go as far as that. I should strongly suspect that as a husband he might prove unsatisfactory in more ways than one."

"Then we can't let her marry him."

"We can't stop her marrying him, if she wants to. And I dare say he won't prove much more unsatisfactory than any other husband she might choose. I shouldn't think he'd beat her, or put arsenic in her coffee, or be rude to her in public. There's a lot to be said, Laura, for having a husband who's agreeable and got good manners."

"Do you know what I think about him? I think he's utterly selfish and—and ruthless."

Mr. Baldock raised his eyebrows.

"I shouldn't wonder if you weren't right."

"Well, then?"

"Yes, but she *likes* the fellow, Laura. She likes him very much. In fact, she's crazy about him. Young Henry mayn't be your cup of tea, and strictly speaking, he isn't my cup of tea, but there's no doubt that he *is* Shirley's cup of tea."

"If she could only see what he's really like!" cried Laura.

"Well, she'll find out," prophesied Mr. Baldock.

"When it's too late! I want her to see what he's like *now!*"

"Dare say it wouldn't make any difference. She means to have him, you know."

"If she could go away somewhere . . . On a cruise or to Switzerland—but everything's so difficult now since the war."

"If you ask me," said Mr. Baldock, "it's never any good trying to stop people marrying each other. Mind you, I'd have a try if there were some serious reason; if he had a wife and five children, or epileptic fits, or was wanted for embezzlement. But shall I tell you exactly what would happen if you did succeed in separating them and sending Shirley off on a cruise or to Switzerland or to a South Sea island?"

"Well?"

Mr. Baldock wagged an emphatic forefinger at her.

"She'd come back having teamed up with another young man of exactly the same kind. People know what they want. Shirley wants Henry, and if she can't get Henry, she'll look around until she finds a young man as like Henry as possible. I've seen it happen again and again. My very best friend was married to a woman who made his life hell on earth, nagged at him, bullied him, ordered him around, never a moment's peace, everybody wondering why he didn't take a hatchet to her. Then he had a bit of luck! She got double pneumonia and died! Six months later, he was looking like a new man. Several really nice women taking an interest in him. Eighteen months later, what has he done? Married a woman who was even a worse bitch than the first one. Human nature's a mystery."

He took a deep breath.

"So stop walking up and down looking like a tragedy

queen, Laura. I've told you already you take life too seriously. You can't run other people's lives for them. Young Shirley has got her own row to hoe. And if you ask me, she can take care of herself a good deal better than you can. It's *you* I'm worried about, Laura. I always have been. . . ."

Chapter four

Henry surrendered as charmingly as he did everything else.

"All right, Laura. If it must be a year's engagement . . . We're in your hands. I dare say it would be very hard on you to part with Shirley without having time to get used to the idea."

"It isn't that—"

"Isn't it?" His eyebrows rose, his smile was faintly ironical. "Shirley's your ewe lamb, isn't she?"

His words left Laura with an uneasy sensation.

The days after Henry had left were not easy to get through.

Shirley was not hostile, but aloof. She was moody, unsettled, and though not openly resentful, a faint air of reproach hung about her. She lived for the arrival of the post, but the post, when it did come, proved unsatisfactory.

Henry was not a letter-writer. His letters were brief scrawls.

"Darling, how's everything? I miss you a lot. I rode in a point-to-point yesterday. Didn't do any good. How's the dragon? Yours always, Henry."

Sometimes a whole week passed without a letter.

Once Shirley went up to London and they had a short and unsatisfactory meeting.

He refused the invitation she brought him from Laura.

"I don't want to come down and stay for the week-end! I want to marry you, and have you to myself for always, not come down and 'walk out' with you under Laura's censorious eye. Don't forget, Laura will turn you against me if she possibly can."

"Oh, Henry, she'd never do anything like that. Never—she hardly ever mentions you."

"Hopes you'll forget about me, I expect."

"As if I should!"

"Jealous old cat."

"Oh, Henry, Laura's a darling."

"Not to me."

Shirley went back home unhappy and restless.

In spite of herself, Laura began to feel worn down.

"Why don't you ask Henry down for a week-end?"

Shirley said sullenly:

"He doesn't want to come."

"Not want to come? How extraordinary."

"I don't think it's so extraordinary. He knows you don't like him."

"I do like him." Laura tried to make her voice convincing.

"Oh, Laura, you don't!"

"I think Henry's a very attractive person."

"But you don't want me to marry him."

"Shirley—that isn't true. I only want you to be quite, quite sure."

"I *am* sure."

Laura cried desperately:

"It's only because I love you so much. I don't want you to make any mistake."

"Well, don't love me so much. I don't *want* to be eternally loved!" She added: "The truth is, you're jealous."

"Jealous?"

"Jealous of Henry. You don't want me to love anyone but you."

"Shirley!"

Laura turned away, her face white.

"You'll never want me to marry *anyone*."

Then, as Laura moved away, walking stiffly, Shirley rushed after her in warm-hearted apology.

"Darling, I didn't mean it, I didn't mean it. I'm a beast. But you always seem so against—Henry."

"It's because I feel he's selfish." Laura repeated the words she had used to Mr. Baldock. "He isn't—he isn't —*kind*. I can't help feeling that in some ways he could be—ruthless."

"Ruthless," Shirley repeated the word thoughtfully without any symptom of distress. "Yes, Laura, in a way you're right. Henry could be ruthless."

She added: "It's one of those things that attracts me in him."

"But think—if you were ill—in trouble—would he look after you?"

"I don't know that I'm so keen on being looked after. I can look after myself. And don't worry about Henry. He loves me."

'Love?' thought Laura. 'What is love? A young man's thoughtless greedy passion? Is Henry's love for her anything more than that? Or is it true, and *am* I jealous?'

She disengaged herself gently from Shirley's clinging arms and walked away deeply disturbed.

'Is it true that I don't want her to marry anybody? Not just Henry? Anybody? I don't think so now, but that's because there is no one else she wants to marry. If someone else were to come along, should I feel the same way as I do now, saying to myself: Not *him*—not *him?* Is it true that I love her too much? Baldy warned me. . . . I love her too much, and so I don't want her to marry—I don't want her to go away—I want to keep her—never to let her go. What have I got against Henry really? Nothing.

I don't know him, I've never known him. He's what he was at first—a stranger. All I do know is that he doesn't like me. And perhaps he's right not to like me.'

On the following day, Laura met young Robin Grant coming out of the vicarage. He took his pipe out of his mouth, greeted her, and strolled beside her into the village. After mentioning that he had just come down from London, he remarked casually:

"Saw Henry last night. Having supper with a glamorous blonde. Very attentive. Mustn't tell Shirley."

He gave a whinny of laughter.

Although Laura recognised the information for exactly what it was, a piece of spite on Robin's part, since he himself had been deeply attracted to Shirley, yet it gave her a qualm.

Henry, she thought, was not a faithful type. She suspected that he and Shirley had come very near to a quarrel on the occasion when they had recently met. Supposing that Henry was becoming friendly with another girl? Supposing that Henry should break off the engagement . . . ?

'That's what you wanted, isn't it?' said the sneering voice of her thoughts. 'You don't want her to marry him? That's the real reason you insisted on a long engagement, isn't it? Come now!'

But she wouldn't really be pleased if Henry broke with Shirley. Shirley loved him. Shirley would suffer. If only she herself was sure, quite sure, that it was for Shirley's good—

'What you mean,' said the sneering voice, 'is for your own good. You want to keep Shirley. . . .'

But she didn't want to keep Shirley that way—not a heart-broken Shirley, not a Shirley unhappy and longing for her lover. Who was she to know what was best, or not best for Shirley?

When she got home, Laura sat down and wrote a letter to Henry:

"Dear Henry," she wrote, "I have been thinking things

over. If you and Shirley really want to marry, I don't feel I ought to stand in your way. . . ."

A month later Shirley, in white satin and lace, was married to Henry in Bellbury parish church by the vicar (with a cold in his head) and given away by Mr. Baldock in a morning coat very much too tight for him. A radiant bride hugged Laura good-bye, and Laura said fiercely to Henry:

"Be good to her, Henry. You *will* be good to her?"

Henry, light-hearted as ever, said: "Darling Laura, what do you think?"

Chapter five

1

"Do you really think it's nice, Laura?"

Shirley, now a wife of three months' standing, asked the question eagerly.

Laura, completing her tour of the flat (two rooms, kitchen, and bath), expressed warm approval.

"I think you've made it lovely."

"It was awful when we moved in. The dirt! We've done most of it ourselves—not the ceilings, of course. It's been such fun. Do you like the red bathroom? It's supposed to be constant hot water, but it isn't usually hot. Henry thought the redness would make it seem hotter—like hell!"

Laura laughed.

"What fun you seem to have had."

"We're frightfully lucky to have found a flat at all. Actually some people Henry knew had it, and they passed it on to us. The only awkward thing is that they don't seem to have paid any bills while they were here. Irate milkmen and furious grocers turn up all the time, but of course it's nothing to do with us. It's rather mean to bilk tradesmen, I think—especially small tradesmen. Henry doesn't think it matters."

"It may make it more difficult for you to get things on credit," said Laura.

"I pay our bills every week," said Shirley virtuously.

"Are you all right for money, darling? The garden's been doing very well lately. If you want an extra hundred."

"What a pet you are, Laura! No, we're all right. Keep it in case there's an emergency—I might have a really serious illness."

"Looking at you, that seems an absurd idea."

Shirley laughed gaily.

"Laura, I'm terribly happy."

"Bless you!"

"Hullo, here's Henry."

Turning the latch-key, Henry entered, and greeted Laura with his usual happy air.

"Hullo, Laura."

"Hullo, Henry. I think the flat's lovely."

"Henry, what's the new job like?"

"New job?" asked Laura.

"Yes. He chucked the other one. It was awfully stuffy. Nothing but sticking on stamps and going to the post."

"I'm willing to start at the bottom," said Henry, "but *not* in the basement."

"What's this like?" Shirley repeated impatiently.

"Promising, I think," said Henry. "Of course it's early days to say."

He smiled charmingly at Laura and told her how very pleased they were to see her.

Her visit went off very well, and she returned to Bellbury feeling that her fears and hesitations had been ridiculous.

2

"But Henry, how *can* we owe so much?"

Shirley spoke in a tone of distress. She and Henry had been married just over a year.

"I know," Henry agreed, "that's what I always feel!

That one *can't* owe all that. Unfortunately," he added sadly, "one always does."

"But how are we going to be able to pay?"

"Oh, one can always stave things off," said Henry vaguely.

"It's a good thing I got that job at the flower place."

"Yes, it is, as it turns out. Not that I want you ever to feel you've got to work. Only if you like it."

"Well, I do like it. I'd be bored to death doing nothing all day. All that happens is that one goes out and buys things."

"I must say," said Henry, picking up a sheaf of accounts rendered, "this sort of thing is very depressing. I do hate Lady Day. One's hardly got over Christmas, and income tax, and all that." He looked down at the topmost bill in his hand. "This man, the one who did the bookcases, is asking for his money in a very rude sort of way. I shall put him straight into the waste-paper-basket." He suited the action to the word, and went on to the next one. " 'Dear sir, we must respectfully draw your attention—' Now that's a nice polite way of putting it."

"So you'll pay that one?"

"I shan't exactly pay it," said Henry, "but I shall file it, ready to pay."

Shirley laughed—

"Henry, I do adore you. But what are we really going to *do?*"

"We needn't worry to-night. Let's go out to dinner somewhere really expensive."

Shirley made a face at him.

"Will that help?"

"It won't help our financial position," Henry admitted. "On the contrary! But it will cheer us up."

3

"Dear Laura,

"Could you possibly lend us a hundred pounds? We're

in a bit of a jam. I've been out of a job for two months now, as you probably know (Laura didn't know), but I'm on the verge of landing something really good. In the meantime we've taken to sneaking out by the service lift to avoid the duns. Really very sorry to sponge like this, but I thought I'd better do the dirty work as Shirley mightn't like to.

> "Yours ever,
> "Henry."

4

"I didn't know you'd borrowed money from Laura!"

"Didn't I tell you?" Henry turned his head lazily.

"No, you didn't." Shirley spoke grimly.

"All right, darling, don't bite my head off. Did Laura tell you?"

"No, she didn't. I saw it in the pass-book."

"Good old Laura, she stumped up without any fuss at all."

"Henry, why did you borrow money from *her*? I wish you hadn't. Anyway, you oughtn't to have done it without telling me about it first."

Henry grinned.

"You wouldn't have let me do it."

"You're quite right. I wouldn't."

"The truth is, Shirley, the position was rather desperate. I got fifty out of old Muriel. And I made sure that I'd get at least a hundred out of Big Bertha—that's my godmother. Unfortunately, she turned me down flat. Feeling her surtax, I gather. Nothing but a lecture. I tried one or two other sources, no good. In the end, it boiled down to Laura."

Shirley looked at him reflectively.

'I've been married two years,' she thought. 'I see now just what Henry's like. He'll never keep a job very long, and he spends money like water. . . .'

She still found it delightful to be married to Henry, but she perceived that it had its disadvantages. Henry had by now had four different jobs. It never seemed difficult for him to get a job—he had a large circle of wealthy friends—but it seemed quite impossible for him to keep a job. Either he got tired of it and chucked it, or it chucked him. Also, Henry spent money like water, and never seemed to have any difficulty in getting credit. His idea of settling his affairs was by borrowing. Henry did not mind borrowing. Shirley did.

She sighed:

"Do you think I'll ever be able to change you, Henry?" she asked.

"Change me?" said Henry, astonished. "Why?"

5

"Hullo, Baldy."

"Why, it's young Shirley." Mr. Baldock blinked at her from the depths of his large shabby arm-chair. "I wasn't asleep," he added aggressively.

"Of course not," said Shirley tactfully.

"Long time since we've seen you down here," said Mr. Baldock. "Thought you'd forgotten us."

"I never forget you!"

"Got your husband with you?"

"Not this time."

"I see." He studied her. "Looking rather thin and pale, aren't you?"

"I've been dieting."

"You women!" He snorted. "In a spot of trouble?" he inquired.

Shirley flared out at him.

"Certainly *not!*"

"All right, all right. I just wanted to know. Nobody ever tells me anything nowadays. And I'm getting deaf. Can't overhear as much as I used to. It makes life very dull."

"Poor Baldy."

"And the doctor says I mustn't do any more gardening —no stooping over flower-beds—blood rushes to my head or something. Damned fool—croak, croak, croak! That's all they do, these doctors!"

"I *am* sorry, Baldy."

"So you see," said Mr. Baldock wistfully. "If you *did* want to tell me anything—well—it wouldn't go any further. We needn't tell Laura."

There was a pause.

"In a way," said Shirley, "I did come to tell you something."

"Thought you did," said Mr. Baldock.

"I thought you might give me—some advice."

"Shan't do that. Much too dangerous."

Shirley paid no attention.

"I don't want to talk to Laura. She doesn't really like Henry. But you like Henry, don't you?"

"I like Henry all right," said Mr. Baldock. "He's a most entertaining fellow to talk to, and he's a nice sympathetic way of listening to an old man blowing off steam. Another thing that I like about him is that he never worries."

Shirley smiled.

"He certainly never worries."

"Very rare in the world nowadays. Everybody I meet has nervous dyspepsia from worrying. Yes, Henry's a pleasant fellow. I don't concern myself about his moral worth as Laura would."

Then he said gently:

"What's he been up to?"

"Do you think I'm a fool, Baldy, to sell out my capital?"

"Is that what you have been doing?"

"Yes."

"Well, when you married, the control of it passed to you. It's yours to do what you like with."

"I know."

"Henry suggest it to you?"

"No. . . . Really no. It was entirely my doing. I didn't want Henry to go bankrupt. I don't think Henry himself would have minded going bankrupt at all. But I would. Do you think I was a fool?"

Mr. Baldock considered.

"In one way, yes, in another way not at all."

"Expound."

"Well, you haven't got very much money. You may need it badly in the future. If you think your attractive husband can be relied upon to provide for you, you can just think again. In that way, you're a fool."

"And the other way?"

"Looking at it the other way, you've paid out your money to buy yourself peace of mind. That may have been quite a wise thing to do." He shot a sharp glance at her. "Still fond of your husband?"

"Yes."

"Is he a good husband to you?"

Shirley walked slowly round the room. Once or twice she ran her finger absently along a table or the back of a chair, and looked at the dust upon it. Mr. Baldock watched her.

She came to a decision at last. Standing by the fireplace, her back turned to him, she said:

"Not particularly."

"In what way?"

In an unemotional voice Shirley said:

"He's having an affair with another woman."

"Serious?"

"I don't know."

"So you came away?"

"Yes."

"Angry?"

"Furious."

"Going back?"

Shirley was silent a moment. Then she said:

"Yes, I am."

"Well," said Mr. Baldock, "it's your life."

Shirley came over to him and kissed the top of his head. Mr. Baldock grunted.

"Thank you, Baldy," she said.

"Don't thank me, I haven't done anything."

"I know," said Shirley. "That's what's so wonderful of you!"

Chapter six

The trouble was, Shirley thought, that one got tired.

She leaned back against the plush of the Underground seat.

Three years ago, she hadn't known what tiredness was. Living in London might be a partial cause. Her work had at first been only part-time, but she now worked full-time at the flower-shop in the West End. After that, there were usually things to buy, and then the journey home in the rush-hour, and then the preparing and cooking of the evening meal.

It was true that Henry appreciated her cooking!

Her eyes closed as she leaned back. Someone trod heavily on her toes and she winced.

She thought: 'But I am tired. . . .'

Her mind went back fitfully over the three and a half years of her married life. . . .

Early bliss . . .

Bills . . .

More bills . . .

Sonia Cleghorn . . .

Rout of Sonia Cleghorn. Henry penitent, charming, affectionate . . .

More money difficulties . . .

Bailiffs . . .

Muriel to the rescue . . .

Expensive and unnecessary but quite delightful holiday at Cannes . . .

The Hon. Mrs. Emlyn Blake . . .

Deliverance of Henry from the toils of Mrs. Emlyn Blake . . .

Henry grateful, penitent, charming . . .

Fresh financial crisis . . .

Big Bertha to the rescue . . .

The Lonsdale girl . . .

Financial worries . . .

Still the Lonsdale girl . . .

Laura . . .

Staving off Laura . . .

Failure to stave off Laura . . .

Row with Laura . . .

Appendicitis. Operation. Convalescence . . .

Return home . . .

Final phase of the Lonsdale girl . . .

Her mind lingered and dwelt on that last item.

She had been resting in the flat. It was the third flat they had lived in, and was filled with furniture bought on the hire purchase system—this last suggested by the incident of the bailiffs.

The bell had rung, and she felt too lazy to get up and open the door. Whoever it was would go away. But whoever it was didn't go away. They rang again and again.

Shirley rose angrily to her feet. She went to the door, pulled it open and stood face to face with Susan Lonsdale.

"Oh, it's you, Sue."

"Yes. Can I come in?"

"Actually I'm rather tired. I've just come back from hospital."

"I know. Henry told me. You poor darling. I've brought you some flowers."

Shirley took the out-thrust bunch of daffodils without any marked expression of gratitude.

"Come in," she said.

She went back to the sofa and put her feet up. Susan Lonsdale sat down in a chair.

"I didn't want to worry you while you were still in hospital," she said. "But I do feel, you know, that we ought to get things settled."

"In what way?"

"Well—Henry."

"What about Henry?"

"Darling, you're not going to be an ostrich, are you? Head in the sand and all that?"

"I don't think so."

"You do know, don't you, that Henry and I have got quite a thing about each other?"

"I should have to be blind and deaf not to know that," said Shirley coldly.

"Yes—yes, of course. And, I mean, Henry's awfully fond of you. He'd hate to upset you in any way. But there it is."

"There what is?"

"What I'm really talking about is divorce."

"You mean that Henry wants a divorce?"

"Yes."

"Then why hasn't he mentioned it?"

"Oh, Shirley darling, you know what Henry's like. He does so hate having to be *definite*. And he didn't want to upset you."

"But you and he want to get married?"

"Yes. I'm *so* glad you understand."

"I suppose I understand all right," said Shirley slowly.

"And you'll tell him that it's all right?"

"I'll talk to him, yes."

"It's awfully sweet of you. I do feel that in the end—"

"Oh, go away," said Shirley. "I'm just out of hospital and I'm *tired*. Go away—at once—do you hear?"

"Well, really," said Susan, rising in some dudgeon. "I do think—well, one might at least be *civilised*."

She went out of the room and the front door banged.

Shirley lay very still. Once a tear crept slowly down her cheek. She wiped it away angrily.

'Three years and a half,' she thought. 'Three years and a half . . . and it's come to this.' And then, suddenly, without being able to help it, she began to laugh. That sentiment sounded so like a line in a bad play.

She didn't know if it was five minutes later or two hours when she heard Henry's key in the door.

He came in looking gay and light-hearted as usual. In his hand was an enormous bunch of long-stemmed yellow roses.

"For you, darling. Nice?"

"Lovely," said Shirley. "I've already had daffodils. Not so nice. Rather cheap and past their prime, as a matter of fact."

"Oh, who sent you those?"

"They weren't *sent*. They were brought. Susan Lonsdale brought them."

"What cheek," said Henry indignantly.

Shirley looked at him in faint surprise.

"What did she come here for?" he asked.

"Don't you know?"

"I suppose I can guess. That girl's becoming a positive pest."

"She came to tell me that you want a divorce."

"That *I* want a divorce? From *you?*"

"Yes. Don't you?"

"Of course I don't," said Henry indignantly.

"You don't want to marry Susan?"

"I should hate to marry Susan."

"She wants to marry you."

"Yes, I'm afraid she does." Henry looked despondent. "She's always ringing me up and writing me letters. I don't know what to do about her."

"Did you tell her you wanted to marry her?"

"Oh, one says things," said Henry vaguely. "Or rather they say things and one agrees. . . . One has to, more or less." He gave her an uneasy smile. "You wouldn't divorce me, would you, Shirley?"

"I might," said Shirley.

"Darling—"

"I'm getting rather—tired, Henry."

"I'm a brute. I've given you a rotten deal." He knelt down beside her. The old alluring smile flashed out. "But I do love you, Shirley. All this other silly nonsense doesn't count. It doesn't mean anything. I'd never want to be married to anyone but you. If you'll go on putting up with me?"

"What did you really feel about Susan?"

"Can't we forget about Susan? She's such a *bore*."

"I'd just like to understand."

"Well—" Henry considered. "For about a fortnight I was mad about her. Couldn't sleep. After that, I still thought she was rather wonderful. After that I thought she was beginning, perhaps, to be just the least bit of a *bore*. And then she quite definitely *was* a bore. And just lately she's been an absolute *pest*."

"Poor Susan."

"Don't worry about Susan. She's got no morals and she's a perfect bitch."

"Sometimes, Henry, I think you're quite heartless."

"I'm not heartless," said Henry indignantly. "I just don't see why people have to cling so. Things are fun if you don't take them seriously."

"Selfish devil!"

"Am I? I suppose I am. You don't really mind, do you, Shirley?"

"I shan't leave you. But I'm rather fed up, all the same. You're not to be trusted over money, and you'll probably go on having these silly affairs with women."

"Oh no, I won't. I swear I won't."

"Oh, Henry, be honest."

"Well, I'll try not to, but do try and understand, Shirley, that none of these affairs mean anything. There's only you."

"I've a good mind to have an affair myself!" said Shirley.

Henry said that he wouldn't be able to blame her if she did.

He then suggested that they should go out somewhere amusing, and have dinner together.

He was a delightful companion all the evening.

Chapter seven

1

Mona Adams was giving a cocktail-party. Mona Adams loved all cocktail-parties, and particularly her own. Her voice was hoarse, since she had had to scream a good deal to be heard above her guests. It was being a very successful cocktail-party.

She screamed now as she greeted a late-comer.

"Richard! How wonderful! Back from the Sahara—or is it the Gobi?"

"Neither. Actually it's the Fezzan."

"Never heard of it. But how good to see you! What a lovely tan. Now who do you want to talk to? Pam, Pam, let me introduce Sir Richard Wilding. You know, the traveller—camels and big game and deserts—those thrilling books. He's just come back from somewhere in—in —Tibet."

She turned and screamed once more at another arrival.

"Lydia! I'd no idea you were back from Paris. *How* wonderful!"

Richard Wilding was listening to Pam, who was saying feverishly:

"I saw you on television—only last night! How thrilling to meet you. Do tell me now—"

But Richard Wilding had no time to tell her anything.

Another acquaintance had borne down upon him.

He fetched up at last, with his fourth drink in his hand, on a sofa beside the loveliest girl he had ever seen.

Somebody had said:

"Shirley, you must meet Richard Wilding."

Richard had at once sat down beside her. He said:

"How exhausting these affairs are! I'd forgotten. Won't you slip away with me, and have a quiet drink somewhere?"

"I'd love to," said Shirley. "This place gets more like a menagerie every minute."

With a pleasing sense of escape, they came out into the cool evening air.

Wilding hailed a taxi.

"It's a little late for a drink," he said, glancing at his watch, "and we've had a good many drinks, anyway. I think dinner is indicated."

He gave the address of a small, but expensive restaurant off Jermyn Street.

The meal ordered, he smiled across the table at his guest.

"This is the nicest thing that's happened to me since I came back from the wilds. I'd forgotten how frightful London cocktail-parties were. Why do people go to them? Why did I? Why do you?"

"Herd instinct, I suppose," said Shirley lightly.

She had a sense of adventure that made her eyes bright. She looked across the table at the bronzed attractive man opposite her.

She was faintly pleased with herself at having snatched away the lion of the party.

"I know all about you," she said. *"And* I've read your books!"

"I don't know anything about you—except that your Christian name is Shirley. What's the rest of it?"

"Glyn-Edwards."

"And you're married." His eyes rested on her ringed finger.

"Yes. And I live in London and work in a flower-shop."

"Do you like living in London, and working in a flower-shop and going to cocktail-parties?"

"Not very much."

"What would you like to do—or be?"

"Let me see." Shirley's eyes half closed. She spoke dreamily. "I'd like to live on an island—an island rather far away from anywhere. I'd like to live in a white house with green shutters and do absolutely nothing all day long. There would be fruit on the island and great curtains of flowers, all in a tangle . . . colour and scent . . . and moonlight every night . . . and the sea would look dark purple in the evenings. . . ."

She sighed and opened her eyes.

"Why does one always choose islands? I don't suppose a real island would be nice at all."

Richard Wilding said softly: "How odd that you should say what you did."

"Why?"

"I could give you your island."

"Do you mean you own an island?"

"A good part of one. And very much the kind of island you described. The sea is wine-dark there at night, and my villa is white with green shutters, and the flowers grow as you describe, in wild tangles of colour and scent, and nobody is ever in a hurry."

"How lovely. It sounds like a dream island."

"It's quite real."

"How can you ever bear to come away?"

"I'm restless. Some day I shall go back there and settle down and never leave it again."

"I think you'd be quite right."

The waiter came with the first course and broke the spell. They began talking lightly of everyday things.

Afterwards Wilding drove Shirley home. She did not ask him to come in. He said: "I hope—we'll soon meet again?"

He held her hand a fraction longer than necessary, and she flushed as she drew it away.

That night she dreamed of an island.

2

"Shirley?"

"Yes?"

"You know, don't you, that I'm in love with you?"

Slowly she nodded.

She would have found it hard to describe the last three weeks. They had had a queer, unreal quality about them. She had walked through them in a kind of permanent abstraction.

She knew that she had been very tired—and that she was still tired, but that out of her tiredness had come a delicious hazy feeling of not being really anywhere in particular.

And in that state of haziness, her values had shifted and changed.

It was as though Henry and everything that pertained to Henry had become dim and rather far away. Whereas Richard Wilding stood boldly in the foreground—a romantic figure rather larger than life.

She looked at him now with grave considering eyes.

He said:

"Do you care for me at all?"

"I don't know."

What *did* she feel? She knew that every day this man came to occupy more and more of her thoughts. She knew that his proximity excited her. She recognised that what she was doing was dangerous, that she might be swept away on a sudden tide of passion. And she knew that, definitely, she didn't want to give up seeing him. . . .

Richard said:

"You're very loyal, Shirley. You've never said anything to me about your husband."

"Why should I?"

"But I've heard a good deal."

Shirley said:

"People will say anything."

"He's unfaithful to you and not, I think, very kind."

"No, Henry's not a kind man."

"He doesn't give you what you ought to have—love, care, tenderness."

"Henry loves me—in his fashion."

"Perhaps. But you want something more than that."

"I used not to."

"But you do now. You want—your island, Shirley."

"Oh! the island. That was just a day-dream."

"It's a dream that could come true."

"Perhaps. I don't think so."

"It *could* come true."

A small chilly breeze came across the river to the terrace on which they were sitting.

Shirley got up, pulling her coat tightly around her.

"We mustn't talk like this any more," she said. "What we're doing is foolish, Richard, foolish and dangerous."

"Perhaps. But you don't care for your husband, Shirley, you care for me."

"I'm Henry's wife."

"You care for *me*."

She said again:

"I'm Henry's wife."

She repeated it like an article of faith.

3

When she got home, Henry was lying stretched out on the sofa. He was wearing white flannels.

"I think I've strained a muscle." He made a faint grimace of pain.

"What have you been doing?"

"Played tennis at Roehampton."

"You and Stephen? I thought you were going to play golf."

"We changed our minds. Stephen brought Mary along, and Jessica Sandys made a fourth."

"Jessica? Is that the dark girl we met at the Archers the other night?"

"Er—yes—she is."

"Is she your latest?"

"Shirley! I told you, I promised you . . ."

"I know, Henry, but what are promises? She *is* your latest—I can see it in your eye."

Henry said sulkily:

"Of course, if you're going to imagine things . . ."

"If I'm going to imagine things," Shirley murmured, "I'd rather imagine an island."

"Why an island?"

Henry sat up on the sofa and said: "I really *do* feel stiff."

"You'd better have a rest to-morrow. A quiet Sunday for a change."

"Yes, that might be nice."

But the following morning Henry declared that the stiffness was passing off.

"As a matter of fact," he said, "we agreed to have a return."

"You and Stephen and Mary—and Jessica?"

"Yes."

"Or just you and Jessica?"

"Oh, all of us," he said easily.

"What a liar you are, Henry."

But she did not say it angrily. There was even a slight smile in her eyes. She was remembering the young man she had met at the tennis party four years ago, and how what had attracted her to him had been his detachment. He was still just as detached.

The shy embarrassed young man who had come to call the following day, and who had sat doggedly talking to

Laura until she herself returned, was the same young man who was now determinedly in pursuit of Jessica.

'Henry,' she thought, 'has really not changed at all.'

'He doesn't want to hurt me,' she thought, 'but he's just like that. He always has to do just what he wants to do.'

She noticed that Henry was limping a little, and she said impulsively:

"I really don't think you ought to go and play tennis—you must have strained yourself yesterday. Can't you leave it until next week-end?"

But Henry wanted to go, and went.

He came back about six o'clock and dropped down on his bed looking so ill that Shirley was alarmed. Notwithstanding Henry's protests, she went and rang up the doctor.

Chapter eight

1

As Laura rose from lunch the following afternoon the telephone rang.

"Laura? It's me, Shirley."

"Shirley? What's the matter? Your voice sounds queer."

"It's Henry, Laura. He's in hospital. He's got polio."

'Like Charles,' thought Laura, her mind rushing back over the years. 'Like Charles . . .'

The tragedy that she herself had been too young to understand acquired suddenly a new meaning.

The anguish in Shirley's voice was the same anguish that her own mother had felt.

Charles had died. Would Henry die?

She wondered. Would Henry die?

2

"Infantile paralysis is the same as polio, isn't it?" she asked Mr. Baldock doubtfully.

"Newer name for it, that's all—why?"

"Henry has gone down with it."

"Poor chap. And you're wondering if he's going to get over it?"

"Well—yes."

"And hoping he won't?"

"Really, really. You make me out a monster."

"Come now, young Laura—the thought was in your mind."

"Horrible thoughts do pass through one's mind," said Laura. "But I wouldn't wish anyone dead—really I wouldn't."

"No," said Mr. Baldock thoughtfully. "I don't believe you would—nowadays—"

"What do you mean—nowadays? Oh, you don't mean that old business of the Scarlet Woman?" She couldn't help smiling at the remembrance. "What I came in to tell you was that I shan't be able to come in and see you every day for a bit. I'm going up to London by the afternoon train—to be with Shirley."

"Does she want you?"

"Of course she'll want me," said Laura indignantly. "Henry's in hospital. She's all alone. She needs someone with her."

"Probably—yes, probably. Quite right. Proper thing to do. It doesn't matter about *me*."

Mr. Baldock, as a semi-invalid, got a lot of pleasure out of an exaggerated self-pity.

"Darling, I'm terribly sorry, but—"

"But Shirley comes first! All right, all right . . . who am I? Only a tiresome old fellow of eighty, deaf, semi-blind—"

"Baldy—"

Mr. Baldock suddenly grinned and closed one eyelid.

"Laura," he said, "you're a push-over for hard luck stories. Anyone who's sorry for himself doesn't need you to be sorry for him as well. Self-pity is practically a full-time occupation."

3

"Isn't it lucky I didn't sell the house?" said Laura.

It was three months later. Henry had not died, but he had been very near death.

"If he hadn't insisted upon going out and playing tennis after the first signs, it wouldn't have been so serious. As it is—"

"It's bad—eh?"

"It's fairly certain that he'll be a cripple for life."

"Poor devil."

"They haven't told him that, of course. And I suppose there's just a chance . . . but perhaps they only say that to cheer up Shirley. Anyway, as I said, it's lucky I haven't sold the house. It's queer—I had a feeling all along that I oughtn't to sell it. I kept saying to myself it was ridiculous, that it was far too big for me, that since Shirley hadn't any children they would never want a house in the country. And I was quite keen to take on this job, running the Children's Home in Milchester. But as it is, the sale hasn't gone through, and I can withdraw and the house will be there for Shirley to bring Henry to when he gets out of hospital. That won't be for some months, of course."

"Does Shirley think that's a good plan?"

Laura frowned.

"No, for some reason she's most reluctant. I think I know why."

She looked up sharply at Mr. Baldock.

"I might as well know—Shirley may have told you what she wouldn't like to tell me. She's got practically none of her own money left, has she?"

"She hasn't confided in me," said Mr. Baldock, "but no, I shouldn't think she had." He added: "I should imagine Henry's gone through pretty well all he ever had, too."

"I've heard a lot of things," said Laura. "From friends of theirs and other people. It's been a terribly unhappy marriage. He's gone through her money, he's neglected her, he's constantly had affairs with other women. Even now, when he's so ill, I can't bring myself to forgive him. How could he treat Shirley like that? If anyone deserved to be happy, Shirley did. She was so full of life and eagerness and—and trust." She got up and walked restlessly about the room. She tried to steady her voice as she went on:

"Why did I ever let her marry Henry? I could have stopped it, you know, or at any rate delayed it so that she would have had time to see what he was like. But she was fretting so—she wanted him. I wanted her to have what she wanted."

"There, there, Laura."

"And it's worse than that. I wanted to show that I wasn't possessive. Just to prove that to myself, I let Shirley in for a lifetime of unhappiness."

"I've told you before, Laura, you worry too much about happiness and unhappiness."

"I can't bear to see Shirley suffer! *You* don't mind, I suppose."

"Shirley, Shirley! It's you I mind about, Laura—always have. Ever since you used to ride round the garden on that fairy-cycle of yours looking as solemn as a judge. You've got a capacity for suffering, and you can't minimise it as some can, by the balm of self-pity. You don't think about yourself at all."

"What do I matter? It isn't *my* husband who's been struck down with infantile paralysis!"

"It might be, by the way you're going on about it! Do you know what I want for you, Laura? Some good everyday happiness. A husband, some noisy, naughty children. You've always been a tragic little thing ever since I've known you—you need the other thing, if you're ever going to develop properly. Don't take the sufferings of the world upon your shoulders—our Lord Jesus Christ did that once for all. You can't live other people's lives for them, not even Shirley's. Help her, yes; but don't *mind* so much."

Laura said, white-faced: "You don't understand."

"You're like all women, have to make such a song and dance about things."

Laura looked at him for a moment in silence, and then turned on her heel and went out of the room.

"Bloody old fool, that's what I am," said Mr. Baldock aloud to himself. "Oh well, I've been and done it now, I suppose."

He was startled when the door opened, and Laura came swiftly through it, and across to his chair.

"You *are* an old devil," she said, and kissed him.

When she went out again, Mr. Baldock lay still and blinked his eyes in some embarrassment.

It had become his habit lately to mutter to himself, and he now addressed a prayer to the ceiling.

"Look after her, Lord," he said. "I can't. And I suppose it's been presumption on my part to try."

4

On hearing of Henry's illness, Richard Wilding had written to Shirley a letter expressing conventional sympathy. A month later he had written again, asking her to see him. She wrote back:

"I don't think we had better meet. Henry is the only reality now in my life. I think you will understand. Goodbye."

To that he replied:

"You have said what I expected you to say. God bless you, my dear, now and always."

So that, Shirley thought, was the end of that. . . .

Henry would live, but what confronted her now were

the practical difficulties of existence. She and Henry had practically no money. When he came out of hospital, a cripple, the first necessity would be a home.

The obvious answer was Laura.

Laura, generous, loving, took it for granted that Shirley and Henry would come to Bellbury. Yet, for some curious reason, Shirley was deeply reluctant to go.

Henry, a bitter rebellious invalid, with no trace of his former light-heartedness, told her she was mad.

"I can't see what you've got against it. It's the obvious thing to do. Thank goodness Laura has never given the house up. There's plenty of room. We can have a whole suite to ourselves, and a bloody nurse or man attendant, too, if I've got to have one. I can't see *what* you are dithering about."

"Couldn't we go to Muriel?"

"She's had a stroke, you know that. She'll probably be having another quite soon. She's got a nurse looking after her and is quite ga-ga, and her income's halved with taxation. It's out of the question. What's wrong with going to Laura? She's offered to have us, hasn't she?"

"Of course she has. Again and again."

"Then that's all right. Why don't you want to go there? You know Laura adores you."

"She loves *me*—but—"

"All right! Laura adores you and doesn't like me! All the more fun for her. She can gloat over my being a helpless cripple and enjoy herself."

"Don't say that, Henry. You know Laura isn't like that."

"What do I care what Laura is like? What do I care about anything. Do you realise what I'm going through? Do you realise what it's like to be helpless, inert, not able to turn over in bed? And what do you care?"

"I care."

"Tied to a cripple! A lot of fun for you!"

"It's all right for me."

"You're like all women, delighted to be able to treat a

man like a child. I'm dependent on you, and I expect you enjoy it."

"Say anything you like to me," said Shirley. "I know just how awful it is for you."

"You don't know in the least. You can't. How I wish I was dead! Why don't these bloody doctors finish one off? It's the only decent thing to do. Go on, say some more soothing, sweet things."

"All right," said Shirley, "I will. This will make you really mad. It's worse for me than it is for you."

Henry glared at her; then, reluctantly, he laughed.

"You called my bluff," he said.

5

Shirley wrote to Laura a month later.

"Darling Laura. It's very good of you to have us. You mustn't mind Henry and the things he says. He's taking it very hard. He's never had to bear anything he didn't want to before, and he gets in the most dreadful rages. It's such an awful thing to happen to anyone like Henry."

Laura's answer, quick and loving, came by return.

Two weeks later, Shirley and her invalid husband came home.

Why, Shirley wondered, as Laura's loving arms went round her, had she ever felt she did not want to come here?

This was her own place. She was back within the circle of Laura's care and protection. She felt like a small child again.

"Laura darling, I'm so glad to be here. . . . I'm so tired . . . so dreadfully tired. . . ."

Laura was shocked by her sister's appearance.

"My darling Shirley, you've been through such a lot . . . don't worry any more."

Shirley said anxiously: "You mustn't mind Henry."

"Of course I shan't mind anything Henry says or does.

How could I? It's dreadful for a man, especially a man like Henry, to be completely helpless. Let him blow off steam as much as he likes."

"Oh, Laura, you *do* understand. . . ."

"Of course I understand."

Shirley gave a sigh of relief. Until this morning, she had hardly realised herself the strain under which she had been living.

Chapter nine

1

Before going abroad again, Sir Richard Wilding went down to Bellbury.

Shirley read his letter at breakfast; and then passed it to Laura, who read it.

"Richard Wilding. Is that the traveller man?"

"Yes."

"I didn't know he was a friend of yours."

"Well—he is. You'll like him."

"He'd better come to lunch. Do you know him well?"

"For a time," said Shirley, "I thought I was in love with him."

"Oh!" said Laura, startled.

She wondered . . .

Richard arrived a little earlier than they had expected. Shirley was up with Henry, and Laura received him, and took him out into the garden.

She thought to herself at once: *'This is the man Shirley ought to have married.'*

She liked his quietness, his warmth and sympathy, and his authoritativeness.

Oh! if only Shirley had never met Henry, Henry with his charm, his instability and his underlying ruthlessness.

Richard enquired politely after the sick man. After the conventional questions and answers, Richard Wilding said:

"I only met him a couple of times. I didn't like him."

And then he asked brusquely:

"Why didn't you stop her marrying him?"

"How could I?"

"You could have found some way."

"Could I? I wonder."

Neither of them felt that their quick intimacy was unusual.

He said gravely:

"I might as well tell you, if you haven't guessed, that I love Shirley very deeply."

"I rather thought so."

"Not that it's any good. She'll never leave the fellow now."

Laura said dryly:

"Could you expect her to?"

"Not really. She wouldn't be Shirley if she did." Then he said: "Do you think she still cares for him?"

"I don't know. Naturally she's dreadfully sorry for him."

"How does he bear up?"

"He doesn't," said Laura sharply. "He's no kind of endurance or fortitude. He just—takes it out of her."

"Swine!"

"We ought to be sorry for him."

"I am in a way. But he always treated her very badly. Everybody knows about it. Did you know?"

"She never said so. Of course I've heard things."

"Shirley's loyal," he said. "Loyal through and through."

"Yes."

After a moment or two's silence Laura said, her voice suddenly harsh:

"You're quite right, you know. I ought to have stopped that marriage. Somehow. She was so young. She hadn't had time. Yes, I made a terrible mess of things."

He said gruffly:

"You'll look after her, won't you?"

"Shirley is the only person in the world I care about."
He said:

"Look, she's coming now."

They both watched Shirley as she came across the lawn towards them.

He said:

"How terribly thin and pale she is. My poor child, my dear brave child . . ."

2

Shirley walked with Richard after lunch by the side of the brook.

"Henry's asleep. I can get out for a little."

"Does he know I'm here?"

"I didn't tell him."

"Are you having a bad time of it?"

"I am—rather. There's nothing I can say or do that's any help to him. That's what's so awful."

"You didn't mind my coming down?"

"Not if it's to say—good-bye."

"It's good-bye all right. You'll never leave Henry now?"

"No. I shall never leave him."

He stopped and took her hands in his.

"Just one thing, my dear. If you need me—at any time —just send the one word: 'Come.' I'll come from the ends of the earth."

"Dear Richard."

"It's good-bye then, Shirley."

He took her in his arms. Her starved and tired body trembled into life. She kissed him wildly, desperately.

"I love you, Richard, I love you, I love you. . . ."

Then she whispered:

"Good-bye. No, don't come with me. . . ."

She tore herself away and ran back towards the house.

Richard Wilding swore under his breath. He cursed Henry Glyn-Edwards and the disease called polio.

3

Mr. Baldock was confined to bed. More than that, he had two nurses in attendance. He loathed them both.

Laura's visits were the only bright spot in his day.

The nurse who was on duty retired tactfully, and Mr. Baldock told Laura all her failings.

His voice rose in a shrill falsetto:

"So damned arch. *'And how are we this morning?'* There's only one of me, I told her. The other one is a damned slab-faced, grinning ape."

"That was very rude of you, Baldy."

"Bah! Nurses are thick-skinned. They don't mind. Held up her finger, and said: 'Naughty, naughty!' *How* I'd like to boil the woman in oil!"

"Now don't get excited. It's bad for you."

"How's Henry? Still playing up?"

"Yes. Henry really is a *fiend!* I try to be sorry for him, but I can't.

"You women! Hard-hearted! Sentimental about dead birds and things like that, and hard as nails when a poor fellow is going through hell."

"It's Shirley who's going through hell. He just—goes for her."

"Naturally. Only person he can take it out of. What's a wife for, if you can't let loose on her in times of trouble?"

"I'm terribly afraid she'll have a breakdown."

Mr. Baldock snorted contemptuously: "Not she. Shirley's tough. She's got guts, Shirley has."

"She's under a terrible strain."

"Yes, I expect so. Well, she would marry the fellow."

"She didn't know he was going to get polio."

"*That* wouldn't have stopped her? What's all this I hear about some romantic swashbuckler coming down here to stage a fond farewell?"

"Baldy, how *do* you get hold of things?"

"Keep my ears open. What's a nurse for, if you can't get the local scandal out of her?"

"It was Richard Wilding, the traveller."

"Oh yes, rather a good chap by all accounts. Made a silly marriage before the war. Glorified Piccadilly tart. Had to get rid of her after the war. Very cut up about it, I believe—silly ass to marry her. These idealists!"

"He's nice—very nice."

"Soft about him?"

"He's the man Shirley ought to have married."

"Oh, I thought maybe you fancied him yourself. Pity."

"I shall never marry."

"Ta-ra-ra-boom-di-ay," said Mr. Baldock rudely.

4

The young doctor said: "You ought to go away, Mrs. Glyn-Edwards. Rest and a change of air is what you need."

"I can't possibly go away."

Shirley was indignant.

"You're very run down. I'm warning you." Dr. Graves spoke impressively. "You'll have a complete breakdown if you're not careful."

Shirley laughed.

"I shall be all right."

The doctor shook his head doubtfully.

"Mr. Glyn-Edwards is a very trying patient," he said.

"If he could only—resign himself a little," said Shirley.

"Yes, he takes things badly."

"You don't think that *I'm* bad for him? That I—well —irritate him?"

"You're his safety-valve. It's hard on you, Mrs. Glyn-Edwards, but you're doing good work, believe me."

"Thank you."

"Continue with the sleeping-pills. It's rather a heavy dose, but he must have rest at night when he works himself up so much. Don't leave them where he can get at them, remember."

Shirley's face grew paler.

"You don't think that he'd—"

"No, no, no," the doctor interrupted her hastily. "I should say definitely not the type to do away with himself. Yes, I know he says he wants to sometimes, but that's just hysteria. No, the danger with this type of drug is that you may wake up in a half-bemused condition, forget you've had your dose and take another. So be careful."

"Of course I will."

She said good-bye and went back to Henry.

Henry was in one of his most unpleasant moods.

"Well, what does he say—everything proceeding satisfactorily! Patient just a *little* irritable, perhaps. No need to worry about *that!*"

"Oh, Henry." Shirley sank down in a chair. "Couldn't you sometimes—be a little kind?"

"Kind—to you?"

"Yes. I'm so tired, so dreadfully tired. If you could just be—sometimes—kind."

"*You've* got nothing to complain about. You're not a twisted mass of useless bones. *You're* all right."

"So you think," said Shirley, "that I'm all right?"

"Did the doctor persuade you to go away?"

"He said I ought to have a change and a rest."

"And you're going, I suppose! A nice week at Bournemouth!"

"No, I'm not going."

"Why not?"

"I don't want to leave you."

"*I* don't care whether you go or not. What use are you to me?"

"I don't seem to be any use," said Shirley dully.

Henry turned his head restlessly.

"Where's my sleeping stuff? You never gave it to me last night."

"Yes, I did."

"You didn't. I woke up and I asked for it. That nurse pretended I'd had it."

"You had had it. You forget."

"Are you going to the vicarage thing to-night?"

"Not if you don't want me to," said Shirley.

"Oh, better go! Otherwise everyone says what a selfish brute I am. I told nurse she could go, too."

"I'll stay."

"You needn't. Laura will look after me. Funny—I've never liked Laura much, but there's something about her that's very soothing when you're ill. There's a sort of—strength."

"Yes. Laura's always been like that. She *gives* you something. She's better than me. I only seem to make you angry."

"You're very annoying sometimes."

"Henry—"

"Yes?"

"Nothing."

When she came in before going out to the vicarage whist drive, she thought at first that Henry was asleep. She bent over him. Tears pricked her eyelids. Then as she turned to go, he plucked at her sleeve.

"Shirley."

"Yes, darling?"

"Shirley—don't hate me."

"Hate you? How could I hate you?"

He muttered: "You're so pale, so thin. . . . I've worn you out. I couldn't help it. . . . I can't help it. I've always hated anything like illness or pain. In the war, I used to think I wouldn't mind being killed, but I could never understand how fellows could bear to be burnt or disfigured or—or maimed."

"I see. I understand. . . ."

"I'm a selfish devil, I know. But I'll get better—better in mind, I mean—even if I never get better in body. We might be able to make a go of it—of everything—if you'll be patient. Just don't leave me."

"I'll never leave you, never."

"I do love you, Shirley. . . . I do. . . . I always
have. There's never really been anyone but you—there
never will be. All these months—you've been so good, so
patient. I know I've been a devil. Say you forgive me."

"There's nothing to forgive. I love you."

"Even if one is a cripple—one might enjoy life."

"We will enjoy life."

"Can't see how!"

With a tremor in her voice, Shirley said:

"Well, there's always eating."

"And drinking," said Henry.

A faint ghost of his old smile showed.

"One might go in for higher mathematics."

"Crossword puzzles for me."

He said:

"I shall be a devil to-morrow, I expect."

"I expect you will. I shan't mind now."

"Where are my pills?"

"I'll give them to you."

He swallowed them obediently.

"Poor old Muriel," he said suddenly.

"What made you think of her?"

"Remembering taking you over there the first time.
You had on a yellow stripy dress. I ought to have gone
and seen old Muriel more often, but she had got to be
such a bore. I hate bores. Now *I'm* a bore."

"No, you're not."

From the hall below, Laura called: "Shirley!"

She kissed him. She ran down the stairs, happiness
surging up in her, happiness and a kind of triumph.

In the hall below, Laura said that nurse had started.

"Oh, am I late? I'll run."

She ran down the drive turning her head to call:

"I've given Henry his sleeping-pills."

But Laura had gone inside again, and was closing the
door.

part 3

Llewellyn - 1956

Chapter one

1

Llewellyn Knox threw open the shutters of the hotel windows and let in the sweet-scented night air. Below him were the twinkling lights of the town, and beyond them the lights of the harbour.

For the first time for some weeks, Llewellyn felt relaxed and at peace. Here, perhaps, in the island, he could pause and take stock of himself and of the future. The pattern of the future was clear in outline, but blurred as to detail. He had passed through the agony, the emptiness, the weariness. Soon, very soon now, he should be able to begin life anew. A simpler, more undemanding life, the life of a man like any other man—with this disadvantage only: he would be beginning it at the age of forty.

He turned back into the room. It was austerely furnished but clean. He washed his face and hands, unpacked his few possessions, and then left his bedroom, and walked down two flights of stairs into the hotel lobby. A clerk was behind a desk there, writing. His eyes came up for a moment, viewed Llewellyn politely, but with no particular interest or curiosity, and dropped once more to his work.

Llewellyn pushed through the revolving doors and went out into the street. The air was warm with a soft, fragrant dampness.

It had none of the exotic languor of the tropics. Its warmth was just sufficient to relax tension. The accentuated tempo of civilisation was left behind here. It was as though in the island one went back to an earlier age, an age where the people went about their business slowly, with due thought, without hurry or stress, but where purpose was still purpose. There would be poverty here, and pain, and the various ills of the flesh, but not the jangled nerves, the feverish haste, the apprehensive thoughts of to-morrow, which are the constant goads of the higher civilisations of the world. The hard faces of the career women, the ruthless faces of mothers, ambitious for their young, the worn grey faces of business executives fighting incessantly so that they and theirs should not go down and perish, the anxious tired faces of multitudes fighting for a better existence to-morrow or even to retain the existence they had—all these were absent from the people who passed him by. Most of them glanced at him, a good-mannered glance that registered him as a foreigner, and then glanced away, resuming their own lives. They walked slowly, without haste. Perhaps they were just taking the air. Even if they were bent upon some particular course, there was no urgency. What was not done to-day could be done to-morrow; friends who awaited their arrival would always wait a little longer, without annoyance.

A grave, polite people, Llewellyn thought, who smiled seldom, not because they were sad, but because to smile one must be amused. The smile here was not used as a social weapon.

A woman with a baby in her arms came up to him and begged in a mechanical, lifeless whine. He did not understand what she said, but her outstretched hand, and the melancholy chant of her words conformed, he thought, to a very old pattern. He put a small coin in her palm and she thanked him in the same mechanical manner and turned away. The baby lay asleep against her shoulder. It was well nourished, and her own face, though worn, was not haggard or emaciated. Probably, he thought, she was not in want, it was simply that begging was her trade. She pursued it mechanically, courteously, and with sufficient success to provide food and shelter for herself and the child.

He turned a corner and walked down a steep street towards the harbour. Two girls, walking together, came up and passed him. They were talking and laughing, and, without turning their heads, it was apparent that they were very conscious of a group of four young men who walked a little distance behind them.

Llewellyn smiled to himself. This, he thought, was the courting pattern of the island. The girls were beautiful with a proud dark beauty that would probably not outlast youth. In ten years, perhaps less, they would look like this elderly woman who was waddling up the hill on her husband's arm, stout, good-humoured, and still dignified in spite of her shapelessness.

Llewellyn went on down the steep, narrow street. It came out on the harbour front. Here there were cafés with broad terraces where people sat and drank little glasses of brightly-coloured drinks. Quite a throng of people were walking up and down in front of the cafés. Here again their gaze registered Llewellyn as a foreigner, but without any overwhelming interest. They were used to foreigners. Ships put in, and foreigners came ashore, sometimes for a few hours, sometimes to stay—though not usually for long, since the hotels were mediocre and not much given to refinements of plumbing. Foreigners, so the glances seemed to say, were not really their concern. Foreigners were extraneous and had nothing to do with the life of the island.

Insensibly, the length of Llewellyn's stride shortened. He had been walking at his own brisk transatlantic pace, the pace of a man going to some definite place, and anxious to get there with as much speed as is consistent with comfort.

But there was, now, no definite place to which he was

going. That was as true spiritually as physically. He was merely a man amongst his fellow kind.

And with that thought there came over him that warm and happy consciousness of brotherhood which he had felt increasingly in the arid wastes of the last months. It was a thing almost impossible to describe—this sense of nearness to, of feeling with, his fellow-men. It had no purpose, no aim, it was as far removed from beneficence as anything could be. It was a consciousness of love and friendliness that gave nothing, and took nothing, that had no wish to confer a benefit or to receive one. One might describe it as a moment of love that embraced utter comprehension, that was endlessly satisfying, and that yet could not, by very reason of what it was, last.

How often, Llewellyn thought, he had heard and said those words: *"Thy loving kindness to us and to all men."*

Man himself could have that feeling, although he could not hold it long.

And suddenly he saw that here was the compensation, the promise of the future, that he had not understood. For fifteen or more years he had been held apart from just that—the sense of brotherhood with other men. He had been a man set apart, a man dedicated to service. But now, now that the glory and the agonising exhaustion were done with, he could become once more a man among men. He was no longer required to serve—only to live.

Llewellyn turned aside and sat down at one of the tables in a café. He chose an inside table against the back wall where he could look over the other tables to the people walking in the street, and beyond them to the lights of the harbour, and the ships that were moored there.

The waiter who brought his order asked in a gentle, musical voice:

"You are American? Yes?"

Yes, Llewellyn said, he was American.

A gentle smile lit up the waiter's grave face.

"We have American papers here. I bring them to you."

Llewellyn checked his motion of negation.

The waiter went away, and came back with a proud expression on his face, carrying two illustrated American magazines.

"Thank you."

"You are welcome, señor."

The periodicals were two years old, Llewellyn noted. That again pleased him. It emphasised the remoteness of the island from the up-to-date stream. Here at least, he thought, there would not be recognition.

His eyes closed for a moment, as he remembered all the various incidents of the last months.

"Aren't you—isn't it? I *thought* I recognised you. . . ."

"Oh, do tell me—you *are* Dr. Knox?"

"You're Llewellyn Knox, aren't you? Oh, I do want to tell you how terribly grieved I was to hear—"

"I knew it must be you! What are your plans, Dr. Knox? Your illness was so terrible. I've heard you're writing a book? I do hope so. Giving us a message?"

And so on, and so on. On ships, in airports, in expensive hotels, in obscure hotels, in restaurants, on trains. Recognised, questioned, sympathised with, fawned upon —yes, that had been the hardest. Women . . . Women with eyes like spaniels. Women with that capacity for worship that women had.

And then there had been, of course, the Press. For even now he was still news. (Mercifully, *that* would not last long.) So many crude brash questions: What are your plans? Would you say now that—? Can I quote you as believing—? Can you give us a message?

A message, a message, always a message! To the readers of a particular journal, to the country, to men and women, to the world—

But he had never had a message to give. He had been a messenger, which was a very different thing. But no one was likely to understand that.

Rest—that was what he had needed. Rest and time. Time to take in what he himself was, and what he should do. Time to take stock of himself. Time to start again, at forty, and live his own life. He must find out what had happened to him, to Llewellyn Knox, the man, during the fifteen years he had been employed as a messenger.

Sipping his little glass of coloured liqueur, looking at the people, the lights, the harbour, he thought that this would be a good place to find out all that. It was not the solitude of a desert he wanted, he wanted his fellow kind. He was not by nature a recluse or an ascetic. He had no vocation for the monastic life. All he needed was to find out who and what was Llewellyn Knox. Once he knew that, he could go ahead and take up life once more.

It all came back, perhaps, to Kant's three questions:

What do I know?

What can I hope?

What ought I to do?

Of these questions, he could answer only one, the second.

The waiter came back and stood by his table.

"They are good magazines?" he asked happily.

Llewellyn smiled.

"Yes."

"They were not very new, I am afraid."

"That does not matter."

"No. What is good a year ago is good now."

He spoke with calm certainty.

Then he added:

"You have come from the ship? The *Santa Margherita?* Out there?"

He jerked his head towards the jetty.

"Yes."

"She goes out again to-morrow at twelve, that is right?"

"Perhaps. I do not know. I am staying here."

"Ah, you have come for a visit? It is beautiful here, so

the visitors say. You will stay until the next ship comes in? On Thursday?"

"Perhaps longer. I may stay here some time."

"Ah, you have business here!"

"No, I have no business."

"People do not usually stay long here, unless they have business. They say the hotels are not good enough, and there is nothing to do."

"Surely there is as much to do here as anywhere else?"

"For us who live here, yes. We have our lives and our work. But for strangers, no. Although we have foreigners who have come here to live. There is Sir Wilding, an Englishman. He has a big estate here—it came to him from his grandfather. He lives here altogether now, and writes books. He is a very celebrated señor, and much respected."

"You mean Sir Richard Wilding?"

The waiter nodded.

"Yes, that is his name. We have known him here many, many years. In the war he could not come, but afterwards he came back. He also paints pictures. There are many painters here. There is a Frenchman who lives in a cottage up at Santa Dolmea. And there is an Englishman and his wife over on the other side of the island. They are very poor, and the pictures he paints are very odd. She carves figures out of stone as well—"

He broke off and darted suddenly forward to a table in the corner at which a chair had been turned up, to indicate that it was reserved. Now he seized the chair and drew it back a little, bowing a welcome at the woman who came to occupy it.

She smiled her thanks at him as she sat down. She did not appear to give him an order, but he went away at once. The woman put her elbows on the table and stared out over the harbour.

Llewellyn watched her with a stirring of surprise.

She wore an embroidered Spanish scarf of flowers on

an emerald green background, like many of the women walking up and down the street, but she was, he was almost sure, either American or English. Her blonde fairness stood out amongst the other occupants of the café. The table at which she was sitting was half obliterated by a great hanging mass of coral-coloured bougainvillaea. To anyone sitting at it, it must have given the feeling of looking out from a cave smothered in vegetation on to the world, and more particularly over the lights of the ships, and their reflections in the harbour.

The girl, for she was little more, sat quite still, in an attitude of passive waiting. Presently the waiter brought her her drink. She smiled her thanks without speaking. Then, her hands cupped round the glass, she continued to stare out over the harbour, occasionally sipping her drink.

Llewellyn noticed the rings on her fingers, a solitaire emerald on one hand, and a cluster of diamonds on the other. Under the exotic shawl she was wearing a plain high-necked black dress.

She neither looked at, nor paid any attention to, the people sitting round her, and none of them did more than glance at her, and even so without any particular attention. It was clear that she was a well-known figure in the café.

Llewellyn wondered who she was. It struck him as a little unusual that a young woman of her class should be sitting there alone, without any companion. Yet she was obviously perfectly at ease and had the air of someone performing a well-known routine. Perhaps a companion would shortly come and join her.

But the time went on, and the girl still sat alone at her table. Occasionally she made a slight gesture with her head, and the waiter brought her another drink.

It was almost an hour later when Llewellyn signalled for his check and prepared to leave. As he passed near her chair, he looked at her.

She seemed oblivious both of him and of her immediate surroundings. She stared now into her glass, now out to sea, and her expression did not change. It was the expression of someone who is very far away.

As Llewellyn left the café and started up the narrow street that led back to his hotel, he had a sudden impulse to go back, to speak to her, to warn her. Now why had that word 'warn' come into his head? Why did he have the idea that she was in danger?

He shook his head. There was nothing he could do about it at the moment, but he was quite sure that he was right.

2

Two weeks later found Llewellyn Knox still on the island. His days had fallen into a pattern. He walked, rested, read, walked again, slept. In the evenings after dinner he went down to the harbour and sat in one of the cafés. Soon he cut reading out of his daily routine. He had nothing more to read.

He was living now with himself only, and that, he knew, was what it should be. But he was not alone. He was in the midst of others of his kind, he was at one with them, even if he never spoke to them. He neither sought nor avoided contact. He had conversations with many people, but none of them meant anything more than the courtesies of fellow human beings. They wished him well, he wished them well, but neither of them wanted to intrude into the other's life.

Yet to this aloof and satisfying friendship there was an exception. He wondered constantly about the girl who came to the café and sat at the table under the bougainvillaea. Though he patronised several different establishments on the harbour front, he came most often to the first one of his choice. Here, on several occasions, he saw the English girl. She arrived always late in the evening and sat at the same table, and he had discovered that she stayed there until almost everyone else had left. Though she was a mystery to him, it was clear to him that she was a mystery to no one else.

One day he spoke of her to the waiter.

"The señora who sits there, she is English?"

"Yes, she is English."

"She lives in the island?"

"Yes."

"She does not come here every evening?"

The waiter said gravely:

"She comes when she can."

It was a curious answer, and Llewellyn thought about it afterwards.

He did not ask her name. If the waiter had wanted him to know her name, he would have told it to him. The boy would have said: "She is the señora so and so, and she lives at such-and-such a place." Since he did not say that, Llewellyn deduced that there was a reason why her name should not be given to a stranger.

Instead he asked:

"What does she drink?"

The boy replied briefly: "Brandy," and went away.

Llewellyn paid for his drink and said good-night. He threaded his way through the tables and stood for a moment on the pavement before joining the evening throng of walkers.

Then, suddenly, he wheeled round and marched with the firm decisive tread of his nationality to the table by the coral bougainvillaea.

"Do you mind," he said, "if I sit down and talk to you for a moment or two?"

Chapter two

1

Her gaze came back very slowly from the harbour lights to his face. For a moment or two her eyes remained wide and unfocused. He could sense the effort she made. She had been, he saw, very far away.

He saw, too, with a sudden quick pity, how very young she was. Not only young in years (she was, he judged, about twenty-three or four), but young in the sense of immaturity. It was as though a normally maturing rosebud had had its growth arrested by frost—it still presented the appearance of normality, but actually it would progress no further. It would not visibly wither. It would just, in the course of time, drop to the ground, unopened. She looked, he thought, like a lost child. He appreciated, too, her loveliness. She was very lovely. Men would always find her lovely, always yearn to help her, to protect her, to cherish her. The dice, one would have said, were loaded in her favour. And yet she was sitting here, staring into unfathomable distance, and somewhere on her easy, assured happy path through life she had got lost.

Her eyes, wide now and deeply blue, assessed him.

She said, a little uncertainly: "Oh—?"

He waited.

Then she smiled.

"Please do."

He drew up a chair and sat.

She asked: "You are American?"

"Yes."

"Did you come off the ship?"

Her eyes went momentarily to the harbour again. There was a ship alongside the quay. There was nearly always a ship.

"I did come on a ship, but not that ship. I've been here a week or two."

"Most people," she said, "don't stay as long as that."

It was a statement, not a question.

Llewellyn gestured to a waiter who came.

He ordered a Curaçao.

"May I order you something?"

"Thank you." she said. And added: "He knows."

The boy bowed his head in assent and went away.

They sat for a moment or two in silence.

"I suppose," she said at last, "you were lonely? There aren't many Americans or English here."

She was, he saw, settling the question of why he had spoken to her.

"No," he said at once. "I wasn't lonely. I find I'm—glad to be alone."

"Oh, one is, isn't one?"

The fervour with which she spoke surprised him.

"I see," he said. "That's why you come here?"

She nodded.

"To be alone. And now I've come and spoilt it?"

"No," she said. "You don't matter. You're a stranger, you see."

"I see."

"I don't even know your name."

"Do you want to?"

"No. I'd rather you didn't tell me. I won't tell you my name, either."

She added doubtfully:

"But perhaps you've been told that already. Everyone in the café knows me, of course."

"No, they haven't mentioned it. They understand, I think, that you would not want it told."

"They do understand. They have, all of them, such wonderful good manners. Not *taught* good manners—the natural thing. I could never have believed till I came here that natural courtesy could be such a wonderful—such a *positive* thing."

The waiter came back with their two drinks. Llewellyn paid him.

He looked over to the glass the girl held cupped in her two hands.

"Brandy?"

"Yes. Brandy helps a lot."

"It helps you to feel alone? Is that it?"

"Yes. It helps me to feel—free."

"And you're not free?"

"Is anybody free?"

He considered. She had not said the words bitterly—as they are usually spoken. She had been asking a simple question.

"*The fate of every man is bound about his neck*—is that what you feel?"

"No, I don't think so. Not quite. I can understand feeling rather like that, that your course was charted out like a ship's, and that you must follow it, again rather like a ship, and that so long as you do, you are all right. But I feel more like a ship that has, quite suddenly, gone off its proper course. And then, you see, you're lost. You don't know where you are, and you're at the mercy of the wind and sea, and you're not free, you're caught in the grip of something you don't understand—tangled up in it all." She added: "What nonsense I'm talking. I suppose it's the brandy."

He agreed.

"It's partly the brandy, no doubt. Where does it take you?"

"Oh, *away* . . . that's all—away. . . ."

"What is it, really, that you have to get away from?"

"Nothing. Absolutely nothing. That's the really—well, wicked part of it. I'm one of the fortunate ones. I've got everything." She repeated sombrely: "Everything. . . . Oh, I don't mean I've not had sorrows, losses, but it's not that. I don't hanker and grieve over the past. I don't resurrect it and live it over again. I don't want to go back, or even forward. I just want to go *away* somewhere. I sit here drinking brandy and presently I'm out there, beyond the harbour, and going farther and farther—into some kind of unreal place that doesn't really exist. It's rather like the dreams of flying you have as a child—no weight —so light—floating."

The wide unfocused stare was coming back to her eyes. Llewellyn sat watching her.

Presently she came to herself with a little start.

"I'm sorry."

"Don't come back. I'm going now." He rose. "May I, now and then, come and sit here and talk to you? If you'd rather not, just say so. I shall understand."

"No, I should like you to come. Good-night. I shan't go just yet. You see, it's not always that I can get away."

2

It was about a week later when they talked together again.

She said as soon as he sat down: "I'm glad you haven't gone away yet. I was afraid you might have gone."

"I shan't go away just yet. It's not time yet."

"Where will you go when you leave here?"

"I don't know."

"You mean—you're waiting for orders?"

"You might put it like that, yes."

She said slowly:

"Last time, when we talked, it was all about me. We didn't talk about you at all. Why did you come here—to the island? Had you a reason?"

"Perhaps it was for the same reason as you drink brandy —to get away, in my case from people."

"People in general, or do you mean special people?"

"Not people in general. I meant really people who know me—or knew me—as I was."

"Did something—happen?"

"Yes, something happened."

She leaned forward.

"Are you like me? Did something happen that put you off course?"

He shook his head with something that was almost vehemence.

"No, not at all. What happened to me was an intrinsic part of the pattern of my life. It had significance and intention."

"But what you said about people—"

"They don't understand, you see. They are sorry for me, and they want to drag me back—to something that's finished."

She wrinkled a puzzled brow.

"I don't quite—"

"I had a job," he said smiling. "Now—I've lost it."

"An important job?"

"I don't know." He was thoughtful. "I thought it was. But one can't really know, you see, what *is* important. One has to learn not to trust one's own values. Values are always relative."

"So you gave up your job?"

"No." His smile flashed out again. "I was sacked."

"Oh." She was taken aback. "Did you—mind?"

"Oh yes, I minded. Anyone would have. But that's all over now."

She frowned at her empty glass. As she turned her head, the boy who had been waiting replaced the empty glass with a full one.

She took a couple of sips, then she said:

"Can I ask you something?"

"Go ahead."

"Do you think happiness is very important?"

He considered.

"That's a very difficult question to answer. If I were to say that happiness is vitally important, and that at the same time it doesn't matter at all, you'd think I was crazy."

"Can't you be a little clearer?"

"Well, it's rather like sex. Sex is vitally important, and yet doesn't matter. You're married?"

He had noticed the slim gold ring on her finger.

"I've been married twice."

"Did you love your husband?"

He left it in the singular, and she answered without quibbling.

"I loved him more than anything in the world."

"When you look back on your life with him, what are the things that come first to your mind, the moments that you will always remember? Are they of the first time you slept together—or are they of something else?"

Laughter came to her suddenly, and a quick enchanting gaiety.

"His hat," she said.

"Hat?"

"Yes. On our honeymoon. It blew away and he bought a native one, a ridiculous straw thing, and I said it would be more suitable for *me*. So I put it on, and then he put on mine—one of those silly bits of nonsense women wear, and we looked at each other and laughed. All trippers change hats, he said, and then he said: 'Good Lord, I do love you. . . .'" Her voice caught. "I'll never forget."

"You see?" said Llewellyn. "Those are the magical moments—the moments of belonging—of everlasting sweetness—not sex. And yet if sex goes wrong, a marriage is completely ruined. So, in the same way, food is important—without it you cannot live, and yet, so long as you *are* fed, it occupies very little of your thoughts. Happiness is one of the foods of life, it encourages growth, it is a great teacher, but it is not the purpose of life, and is, in itself, not ultimately satisfying."

He added gently:

"Is it happiness that you want?"

"I don't know. I ought to be happy. I have everything to make me happy."

"But you want something more?"

"*Less,*" she said quickly, "I want *less* out of life. It's too much—it's all too much."

She added, rather unexpectedly:

"It's all so *heavy.*"

They sat for some time in silence.

"If I knew," she said at last, "if I knew in the least what I really wanted, instead of just being so negative and idiotic."

"But you do know what you want; you want to escape. Why don't you, then?"

"Escape?"

"Yes. What's stopping you? Money?"

"No, it's not money. I have money—not a great deal, but sufficient."

"What is it then?"

"It's so many things. You wouldn't understand." Her lips twisted in a sudden, ruefully humorous smile. "It's like Tchekov's three sisters, always moaning about going to Moscow; they never go, and never will, although I suppose they *could* just have gone to the station and taken a train to Moscow any day of their lives! Just as I could buy a ticket and sail on that ship out there, that sails tonight."

"Why don't you?"

He was watching her.

"You think you know the answer," she said.

He shook his head.

"No, I don't know the answer. I'm trying to help you find it."

"Perhaps I'm like Tchekov's three sisters. Perhaps I don't really want to go."

"Perhaps."

"Perhaps escape is just an idea that I play with."

"Possibly. We all have fantasies that help us to bear the lives we live."

"And escape is my fantasy?"

"I don't know. *You* know."

"I don't know anything—anything at all. I had every chance, I did the wrong thing. And then, when one has done the wrong thing, one has to stick to it, hasn't one?"

"I don't know."

"Must you go *on* saying that over and over?"

"I'm sorry, but it's true. You're asking me to come to a conclusion on something I know nothing about."

"It was a general principle."

"There isn't such a thing as a general principle."

"Do you mean"—she stared at him—"that there isn't such a thing as absolute right and wrong?"

"No, I didn't mean that. Of course there's absolute right and wrong, but that's a thing so far beyond our knowledge and comprehension, that we can only have the dimmest apprehension of it."

"But surely one knows what is right?"

"You have been taught it by the accepted canons of the day. Or, going further, you can feel it of your own instinctive knowledge. But even that's a long way off. People were burned at the stake, not by sadists or brutes, but by earnest and high-minded men, who believed that what they did was right. Read some of the law cases in ancient Greece, of a man who refused to let his slaves be tortured so as to get at the truth, as was the prevalent custom. He was looked upon as a man who deliberately obscured justice. There was an earnest God-fearing clergyman in the States who beat his three-year-old son, whom he loved, to death, because the child refused to say his prayers."

"That's all horrible!"

"Yes, because time has changed our ideas."

"Then, what can we do?"

Her lovely bewildered face bent towards him.

"Follow your pattern, in humility—and hope."

"Follow one's pattern—yes, I see that, but my pattern —it's wrong somehow." She laughed. "Like when you're knitting a jumper and you've dropped a stitch a long way back."

"I wouldn't know about that," he said. "I've never knitted."

"Why wouldn't you give me an opinion just now?"

"It would only have been an opinion."

"Well?"

"And it might have influenced you. . . . I should think you're easily influenced."

Her face grew sombre again.

"Yes. Perhaps that's what was wrong."

He waited for a moment or two, then he said in a matter-of-fact voice:

"What exactly *is* wrong?"

"Nothing." She looked at him despairingly. "Nothing. I've got everything any woman could want."

"You're generalising again. You're not any woman. You're you. Have *you* got everything you want?"

"Yes, yes, *yes!* Love and kindness and money and luxury, and beautiful surroundings and companionship—everything. All the things that I would have chosen for myself. No, it's *me*. There's something wrong with *me*."

She looked at him defiantly. Strangely enough, she was comforted when he answered matter-of-factly:

"Oh yes. There's something wrong with *you*—that's very clear."

3

She pushed her brandy-glass a little way away from her.

She said: "Can I talk about myself?"

"If you like."

"Because if I did, I might just see where—it all went wrong. That would help, I think."

"Yes. It might help."

"It's all been very nice and ordinary—my life, I mean. A happy childhood, a lovely home. I went to school and did all the ordinary things, and nobody was ever nasty to me; perhaps if they had been, it would have been better for me. Perhaps I was a spoiled brat—but no, I don't really think so. And I came home from school and played tennis and danced, and met young men, and wondered what job to take up—all the usual things."

"Sounds straightforward enough."

"And then I fell in love and married." Her voice changed slightly.

"And lived happily . . ."

"No." Her voice was thoughtful. "I loved him, but I was unhappy very often." She added: "That's why I asked you if happiness really mattered."

She paused, and then went on:

"It's so hard to explain. I wasn't very happy, but yet in a curious way it was all right—it was what I'd chosen, what I wanted. I didn't—go into it with my eyes shut. Of course I idealised him—one does. But I remember now, waking up very early one morning—it was about five o'clock, just before dawn. That's a cold, truthful time, don't you think? And I knew then—*saw*, I mean—what the future would become, I knew I shouldn't be really happy, I saw what he was like, selfish and ruthless in a gay kind of charming way, but I saw, too, that he was charming, and gay and light-hearted—and that I loved him, and that no one else would do, and that I would rather be unhappy, married to him, than smug and comfortable without him. And I thought I could, with luck, and if I wasn't too stupid, make a go of it. I accepted the fact that I loved him more than he would ever love me, and that I mustn't—ever—ask him for more than he wanted to give."

She stopped a moment, and then went on:

"Of course I didn't put it to myself as clearly as all that. I'm describing now what was then just a feeling. But it was *real*. I went back again to thinking him wonderful and inventing all sorts of noble things about him that weren't in the least true. But I'd had my *moment*—the moment when you do see what lies ahead of you, and you can turn back or go on. I did think in those cold early morning minutes when you see how difficult and —yes—frightening things are—I did think of turning back. But instead I chose to go on."

He said very gently:

"And you regret—?"

"No, *no!*" She was vehement. "I've never regretted. Every minute of it was worthwhile! There's only one thing to regret—that he died."

The deadness was gone from her eyes now. It was no longer a woman drifting away from life towards fairyland, who leaned forward facing him across the table. It was a woman passionately alive.

"He died too soon," she said. "What is it Macbeth says? *'She should have died hereafter.'* That's what I feel about him. He should have died hereafter."

He shook his head.

"We all feel that when people die."

"Do we? I wouldn't know. I know he was ill. I realise he'd have been a cripple for life. I realise he bore it all badly and hated his life, and took it out on everybody and principally on me. But he didn't *want* to die. In spite of everything he didn't want to die. That's why I resent it so passionately for him. He'd what amounts to a genius for living—even half a life, even a quarter, he would have enjoyed. Oh!" She raised her arms passionately. "I *hate* God for making him die."

She stopped then, and looked at him doubtfully. "I shouldn't have said that—that I hated God."

He said calmly: "It's much better to hate God than to hate your fellow-men. You can't hurt God."

"No. But He can hurt you."

"Oh no, my dear. We hurt each other, and hurt ourselves."

"And make God our scapegoat?"

156

"That is what He has always been. He bears our burdens—the burden of our revolts, of our hates, yes, and of our love."

Chapter three

1

In the afternoons, Llewellyn had formed the habit of going for long walks. He would start up from the town on a widely curving, zig-zagging road that led steadily upwards until the town and the bay lay beneath him, looking curiously unreal in the stillness of the afternoon. It was the hour of the siesta, and no gaily-coloured dots moved on the water-front, or on the occasionally glimpsed roads and streets. Up here on the hills, the only human creatures Llewellyn met were goat-herds, little boys who wandered singing to themselves in the sunshine, or sat playing games of their own with little heaps of stones. These would give Llewellyn a grave good afternoon, without curiosity. They were accustomed to foreigners who strode energetically along, their shirts open at the neck, perspiring freely. Such foreigners were, they knew, either writers or painters. Though not numerous, they were, at least, no novelty. As Llewellyn had no apparatus of canvas or easel or even sketch-book with him, they put him down as a writer, and said to him politely: "Good-afternoon."

Llewellyn returned their greetings and strode on.

He had no particular purpose in his wandering. He observed the scenery, but it had for him no special significance. Significance was within him, not yet clear and recognised, but gradually gaining form and shape.

A path led him through a grove of bananas. Once within its green spaces, he was struck by how immediately all sense of purpose or direction had to be abandoned. There was no knowing how far the bananas extended, and where or when he would emerge. It might be a tiny path, or it might extend for miles. One could only continue on one's way. Eventually one would emerge at the point where the path had led one. That point was already in existence, fixed. He himself could not determine it. What he could determine was his own progression—his feet trod the path as a result of his own will and purpose. He could turn back or he could continue. He had the freedom of his own integrity. To travel hopefully . . .

Presently with almost disconcerting suddenness, he came out from the green stillness of the bananas on to a bare hill-side. A little below him, to one side of a path that zig-zagged down the side of a hill, a man sat painting at an easel.

His back was to Llewellyn, who saw only the powerful line of shoulders outlined beneath the thin yellow shirt and a broad-brimmed battered felt hat stuck on the back of the painter's head.

Llewellyn descended the path. As he drew abreast, he slackened speed, looking with frank interest at the work proceeding on the canvas. After all, if a painter settled himself by what was evidently a well-trodden path, it was clear that he had no objection to being overlooked.

It was a vigorous bit of work, painted in strong bands of colour, laid on with an eye to broad effect, rather than detail. It was a pleasing piece of craftsmanship, though without deep significance.

The painter turned his head sideways and smiled.

"Not my life work," he said cheerfully. "Just a hobby."

He was a man of perhaps between forty and fifty, with dark hair just tinged with grey. He was handsome, but Llewellyn was conscious not so much of his good looks as of the charm and magnetism of his personality. There was a warmth to him, a kindly radiating vitality that made him a person who, if met only once, would not easily be forgotten.

"It's extraordinary," said the painter meditatively, "the pleasure it gives one to squeeze out rich, luscious colours on to a palette and splash 'em all over a canvas! Sometimes one knows what one's trying to do, and sometimes one doesn't, but the pleasure is always there." He gave a quick upward glance. "You're not a painter?"

"No. I just happen to be staying here."

"I see." The other laid a streak of rose colour unexpectedly on the blue of his sea. "Funny," he said. "That looks good. I thought it might. Inexplicable!"

He dropped his brush on to the palette, sighed, pushed his dilapidated hat farther back on his head, and turned slightly sideways to get a better view of his companion. His eyes narrowed in sudden interest.

"Excuse me," he said, "but aren't you Dr. Llewellyn Knox?"

2

There was a moment's swift recoil, not translated into physical motion, before Llewellyn said tonelessly:

"That's so."

He was aware a moment later of how quick the other man's perceptions were.

"Stupid of me," he said. "You had a breakdown in health, didn't you? And I suppose you came here to get away from people. Well, you needn't worry. Americans seldom come to the island, the local inhabitants aren't interested in anybody but their own cousins and their cousins' cousins, and the births, deaths and marriages of same, and I don't count. I live here."

He shot a quick glance at the other.

"That surprise you?"

"Yes, it does."

"Why?"

"Just to live—I should not have thought you would be contented with that."

"You're right, of course. I didn't come here originally to live. I was left a big estate here by a great-uncle of mine. It was in rather a bad way when I took it on. Gradually it's beginning to prosper. Interesting." He added: "My name's Richard Wilding."

Llewellyn knew the name; traveller, writer—a man of varied interests and widely diffused knowledge in many spheres, archaeology, anthropology, entomology. He had heard it said of Sir Richard Wilding that there was no subject of which he had not some knowledge, yet withal he never pretended to be a professional. The charm of modesty was added to his other gifts.

"I have heard of you, of course," said Llewellyn. "Indeed, I have enjoyed several of your books very much indeed."

"And I, Dr. Knox, have attended your meetings—one of them; that is to say, at Olympia a year and a half ago."

Llewellyn looked at him in some surprise.

"That seems to surprise you," said Wilding, with a quizzical smile.

"Frankly, it does. Why did you come, I wonder?"

"To be frank, I came to scoff, I think."

"That does not surprise me."

"It doesn't seem to annoy you, either."

"Why should it?"

"Well, you're human, and you believe in your mission —or so I assume."

Llewellyn smiled a little.

"Oh yes, you can assume that."

Wilding was silent for a moment. Then he said, speaking with a disarming eagerness:

"You know, it's extraordinarily interesting to me to meet you like this. After attending the meeting, the thing I desired most was actually to meet you."

"Surely there would have been no difficulty about doing that?"

"In a certain sense, no. It would have been obligatory on you! But I wanted to meet you on very different terms—on such terms that you could, if you wanted to, tell me to go to the devil."

Llewellyn smiled again.

"Well, those conditions are fulfilled now. I have no longer any obligations."

Wilding eyed him keenly.

"I wonder now, are you referring to health or to viewpoint?"

"It's a question, I should say, of function."

"Hm—that's not very clear."

The other did not answer.

Wilding began to pack up his painting things.

"I'd like to explain to you just how I came to hear you at Olympia. I'll be frank, because I don't think you're the type of man to be offended by the truth when it's not offensively meant. I disliked very much—still do—all that that meeting at Olympia stood for. I dislike more than I can tell you the idea of mass religion relayed, as it were, by loud-speaker. It offends every instinct in me."

He noted the amusement that showed for a moment on Llewellyn's face.

"Does that seem to you very British and ridiculous?"

"Oh, I accept it as a point of view."

"I came therefore, as I have told you, to scoff. I expected to have my finer susceptibilities outraged."

"And you remained to bless?"

The question was more mocking than serious.

"No. My views in the main are unchanged. I dislike seeing God put on a commercial basis."

"Even by a commercial people in a commercial age? Do we not always bring to God the fruits in season?"

"That is a point, yes. No, what struck me very forcibly was something that I had not expected—your own very patent sincerity."

Llewellyn looked at him in genuine surprise.

"I should have thought that might be taken for granted."

"Now that I have met you, yes. But it might have been a racket—a comfortable and well-paid racket. There are political rackets, so why not religious rackets? Granted you've got the gift of the gab, which you certainly have, I imagine it's a thing you could do very well out of, if you put yourself over in a big way or could get someone to do that for you. The latter, I should imagine?"

It was half a question.

Llewellyn said soberly: "Yes, I was put over in a big way."

"No expense spared?"

"No expense spared."

"That, you know, is what intrigues me. How you could stand it? That is, after I had seen and heard you."

He slung his painting things over his shoulder.

"Will you come and dine with me one night? It would interest me enormously to talk to you. That's my house down there on the point. The white villa with the green shutters. But just say so, if you don't want to. Don't bother to find an excuse."

Llewellyn considered for a moment before he replied: "I should like to come very much."

"Good. To-night?"

"Thank you."

"Nine o'clock. Don't change."

He strode away down the hill-side. Llewellyn stood for a moment looking after him, then he resumed his own walk.

3

"So you go to the villa of the Señor Sir Wilding?"

The driver of the ramshackle victoria was frankly interested. His dilapidated vehicle was gaily adorned with painted flowers, and his horse was decked with a necklace of blue beads. The horse, the carriage and the driver seemed equally cheerful and serene.

"He is very sympathetic, the Señor Sir Wilding," he

said. "He is not a stranger here. He is one of us. Don Estobal, who owned the villa and the land, he was old, very old. He let himself be cheated, all day long he read books, and more books came for him all the time. There are rooms in the villa lined with books to the ceiling. It is incredible that a man should want so many books. And then he dies, and we all wonder, will the villa be sold? But then Sir Wilding comes. He has been here as a boy, often, for Don Estobal's sister married an Englishman, and her children and her children's children would come here in the holidays from their schools. But after Don Estobal's death the estate belongs to Sir Wilding, and he comes here to inherit, and he starts at once to put all in order, and he spends much money to do so. But then there comes the war, and he goes away for many years, but he says always that if he is not killed, he will return here—and so at last he has done so. Two years ago it is now since he returned here with his new wife, and has settled here to live."

"He has married twice then?"

"Yes." The driver lowered his voice confidentially. "His first wife was a bad woman. She was beautiful, yes, but she deceived him much with other men—yes, even here in the island. He should not have married her. But where women are concerned, he is not clever—he believes too much."

He added, almost apologetically:

"A man should know whom to trust, but Sir Wilding does not. He does not know about women. I do not think he will ever learn."

Chapter four

His host received Llewellyn in a long, low room, lined to the ceiling with books. The windows were thrown open, and from some distance below there came the gentle murmur of the sea. Drinks were set on a low table near the window.

Wilding greeted him with obvious pleasure, and apologised for his wife's absence.

"She suffers badly from migraine," he said. "I hoped that with the peace and quiet of her life out here it might improve, but it hasn't done so noticeably. And doctors don't really seem to have the answer for it."

Llewellyn expressed his sorrow politely.

"She's been through a lot of trouble," said Wilding. "More than any girl should be asked to bear. And she was so young—still is."

Reading his face, Llewellyn said gently:

"You love her very much."

Wilding sighed:

"Too much, perhaps, for my own happiness."

"And for hers?"

"No love in the world could be too much to make up to her for all she has suffered."

He spoke vehemently.

Between the two men there was already a curious sense

of intimacy which had, indeed, existed from the first moment of their meeting. It was as though the fact that neither of them had anything in common with the other —nationality, upbringing, way of life, beliefs—made them therefore ready to accept each other without the usual barriers of reticence or conventionality. They were like men marooned together on a desert island, or afloat on a raft for an indefinite period. They could speak to each other frankly, almost with the simplicity of children.

Presently they went into dinner. It was an excellent meal, beautifully served, of a very simple character. There was wine which Llewellyn refused.

"If you'd prefer whisky . . ."

The other shook his head.

"Thank you— just water."

"Is that—excuse me—a principle with you?"

"No. Actually it is a way of life that I need no longer follow. There is no reason—now—why I should not drink wine. Simply I am not used to it."

As he uttered the word 'now', Wilding raised his head sharply. He looked intensely interested. He almost opened his mouth to speak, then rather obviously checked himself, and began to talk of extraneous matters. He was a good talker, with a wide range of subjects. Not only had he travelled extensively, and in many unknown parts of the globe, but he had the gift of making all he himself had seen and experienced equally real to the person who was listening to him.

If you wanted to go to the Gobi Desert, or to the Fezzan, or to Samarkand, when you had talked of those places with Richard Wilding, you had been there.

It was not that he lectured, or in any way held forth. His conversation was natural and spontaneous.

Quite apart from his enjoyment of Wilding's talk, Llewellyn found himself increasingly interested by the personality of the man himself. His charm and magnetism were undeniable, and they were also, so Llewellyn judged, entirely unself-conscious. Wilding was not exerting himself to radiate charm; it was natural to him. He was a man of parts, too, shrewd, intellectual without arrogance, a man with a vivid interest in ideas and people as well as in places. If he had chosen to specialise in some particular subject—but that, perhaps, was his secret: he never had so chosen, and never would. That left him human, warm, and essentially approachable.

And yet, it seemed to Llewellyn, he had not quite answered his own question—a question as simple as that put by a child. "Why do I like this man so much?"

The answer was not in Wilding's gifts. It was something in the man himself.

And suddenly, it seemed to Llewellyn, he got it. It was because, with all his gifts, the man himself was fallible. He was a man who could, who would, again and again prove himself mistaken. He had one of those warm, kindly emotional natures that invariably meet rebuffs because of their untrustworthiness in making judgments.

Here was no clear, cool, logical appraisal of men and things; instead there were warm-hearted impulsive beliefs, mainly in people, which were doomed to disaster because they were based on kindliness always rather than on fact. Yes, the man was fallible, and being fallible, he was also lovable. Here, thought Llewellyn, is someone whom I should hate to hurt.

They were back again now in the library, stretched out in two big arm-chairs. A wood fire had been lit, more to convey the sense of a hearth, than because it was needed. Outside the sea murmured, and the scent of some night-blooming flower stole into the room.

Wilding was saying disarmingly:

"I'm so interested, you see, in people. I always have been. In what makes them tick, if I might put it that way. Does that sound very cold-blooded and analytical?"

"Not from you. You wonder about your fellow human beings because you care for them and are therefore interested in them."

"Yes, that's true." He paused. Then he said: "If one

can help a fellow human being, that seems to me the most worthwhile thing in the world."

"If," said Llewellyn.

The other looked at him sharply.

"That seems oddly sceptical, coming from you."

"No, it's only a recognition of the enormous difficulty of what you propose."

"Is it so difficult? Human beings want to be helped."

"Yes, we all tend to believe that in some magical manner others can attain for us what we can't—or don't want to—attain for ourselves."

"Sympathy—and belief," said Wilding earnestly. "To believe the best of someone is to call the best into being. People respond to one's belief in them. I've found that again and again."

"For how long?"

Wilding winced, as though something had touched a sore place in him.

"You can guide a child's hand on the paper, but when you take your hand away the child still has to learn to write himself. Your action may, indeed, have delayed the process."

"Are you trying to destroy my belief in human nature?"

Llewellyn smiled as he said:

"I think I'm asking you to have pity on human nature."

"To encourage people to give of their best—"

"Is forcing them to live at a very high altitude; to keep up being what someone expects you to be is to live under a great strain. Too great a strain leads eventually to collapse."

"Must one then expect the worst of people?" asked Wilding satirically.

"One should recognise that probability."

"And you a man of religion!"

Llewellyn smiled:

"Christ told Peter that before the cock crew, he would have denied Him thrice. He knew Peter's weakness of character better than Peter himself knew it, and loved him none the less for it."

"No," said Wilding, with vigour, "I can't agree with you. In my own first marriage"—he paused, then went on —"my wife was—could have been—a really fine character. She'd got into a bad set; all she needed was love, trust, belief. If it hadn't been for the war—" He stopped. "Well, it was one of the lesser tragedies of war. I was away, she was alone, exposed to bad influences."

He paused again before saying abruptly: "I don't blame her. I make allowances—she was the victim of circumstances. It broke me up at the time. I thought I'd never feel the same man again. But time heals. . . ."

He made a gesture.

"Why I should tell you the history of my life I don't know. I'd much rather hear about your life. You see, you're something absolutely new to me. I want to know the 'why' and 'how' of you. I was impressed when I came to that meeting, deeply impressed. Not because you swayed your audience—that I can understand well enough. Hitler did it. Lloyd George did it. Politicians, religious leaders and actors, they can all do it in a greater or lesser degree. It's a gift. No, I wasn't interested in the *effect* you were having, I was interested in *you*. Why was this particular thing worthwhile to you?"

Llewellyn shook his head slowly.

"You are asking me something that I do not know myself."

"Of course, a strong religious conviction." Wilding spoke with slight embarrassment, which amused the other.

"You mean, belief in God? That's a simpler phrase, don't you think? But it doesn't answer your question. Belief in God might take me to my knees in a quiet room. It doesn't explain what you are asking me to explain. Why the public platform?"

Wilding said rather doubtfully:

"I can imagine that you might feel that in that way you could do more good, reach more people."

Llewellyn looked at him in a speculative manner.

"From the way you put things, I am to take it that you yourself are not a believer?"

"I don't know, I simply don't know. Yes, I do believe in a way. I want to believe . . . I certainly believe in the positive virtues—kindness, helping those who are down, straight dealing, forgiveness."

Llewellyn looked at him for some moments.

"The Good Life," he said. "The Good Man. Yes, that's much easier than to attempt the recognition of God. That's *not* easy, it's very difficult, and very frightening. And what's even more frightening is to stand up to God's recognition of *you*."

"Frightening?"

"It frightened Job." Llewellyn smiled suddenly: "He hadn't an idea, you know, poor fellow, as to what it was all about. In a world of nice rules and regulations, rewards and punishments, doled out by Almighty God strictly according to merit, he was singled out. (Why? We don't know. Some quality in him in advance of his generation? Some power of perception given him at birth?) Anyway, the others could go on being rewarded and punished, but Job had to step into what must have seemed to him a new dimension. After a meritorious life, he was *not* to be rewarded with flocks and herds. Instead, he was to pass through unendurable suffering, to lose his beliefs, and see his friends back away from him. He had to endure the whirlwind. And then, perhaps, having been groomed for stardom, as we say in Hollywood, he could hear the voice of God. And all for what? So that he could begin to recognise what God actually *was*. 'Be still and know that I am God.' A terrifying experience. The highest pinnacle that man, so far, had reached. It didn't, of course, last long. It couldn't. And he probably made a fine mess trying to tell about it, because there wasn't the vocabulary, and you can't describe in terrestrial terms an experience that is spiritual. And whoever tidied up the end of the Book of Job hadn't an idea what it was all about either, but he made it have a good moral happy ending, according to the lights of the time, which was very sensible of him."

Llewellyn paused.

"So you see," he said, "that when you say that perhaps I chose the public platform because I could do more good, and reach more people, that simply is miles off the course. There's no numerical value in reaching people as such, and 'doing good' is a term that really hasn't any significance. What *is* doing good? Burning people at the stake to save their souls? Perhaps. Burning witches alive because they are evil personified? There's a very good case for it. Raising the standard of living for the unfortunate? We think nowadays that that is important. Fighting against cruelty and injustice?"

"Surely you agree with that?"

"What I'm getting at is that these are all problems of *human* conduct. What is good to do? What is right to do? What is wrong to do? We are human beings, and we have to answer those questions to the best of our ability. We have our life to live in this world. But all that has nothing to do with spiritual experience."

"Ah," said Wilding. "I begin to understand. I think you yourself went through some such experience. How did it come about? What happened? Did you always know, even as a child——?"

He did not finish the question.

"Or had you," he said slowly, "no idea?"

"I had no idea," said Llewellyn.

Chapter five

1

No idea . . . Wilding's question had taken Llewellyn back into the past. A long way back.

He himself as a child . . .

The pure clear tang of the mountain air was in his nostrils. The cold winters, the hot, arid summers. The small closely-knit community. His father, that tall, gaunt Scot, austere, almost grim. A God-fearing, upright man, a man of intellect, despite the simplicity of his life and calling, a man who was just and inflexible, and whose affections, though deep and true, were not easily shown. His dark-haired Welsh mother, with the lilting voice which made her most ordinary speech sound like music . . . Sometimes, in the evenings, she would recite in Welsh the poem that her father had composed for the Eisteddfod long years ago. The language was only partly understood by her children, the meaning of the words remained obscure, but the music of the poetry stirred Llewellyn to vague longings for he knew not what. A strange intuitive knowledge his mother had, not intellectual like his father, but a natural innate wisdom of her own.

Her dark eyes would pass slowly over her assembled children and would linger longest on Llewellyn, her first-born, and in them would be an appraisement, a doubt, something that was almost fear.

That look would make the boy himself restless. He

would ask apprehensively: "What is it, Mother? What have I done?"

Then she would smile, a warm, caressing smile, and say:

"Nothing, bach. It's my own good son you are."

And Angus Knox would turn his head sharply and look, first at his wife, and then at the boy.

It had been a happy childhood, a normal boy's childhood. Not luxurious, indeed spartan in many ways. Strict parents, a disciplined way of life. Plenty of home chores, responsibility for the four younger children, participation in the community activities. A godly but narrow way of life. And he fitted in, accepted it.

But he had wanted education, and here his father had encouraged him. He had the Scot's reverence for learning, and was ambitious for this eldest son of his to become something more than a mere tiller of the soil.

"I'll do what I can to help you, Llewellyn, but that will not be much. You'll have to manage mostly for yourself."

And he had done so. Encouraged by his teacher, he had gone ahead and put himself through college. He had worked in vacations, waiting in hotels and camps, he had done evening work washing dishes.

With his father he had discussed his future. Either a teacher or a doctor, he decided. He had had no particular sense of vocation, but both careers seemed to him congenial. He finally chose medicine.

Through all these years, was there no hint of dedication, of special mission? He thought back, trying to remember.

There had been *something* . . . yes, looking back from to-day's viewpoint, there had been something. Something not understood by himself at the time. A kind of fear—that was the nearest he could get to it. Behind the normal façade of daily life, a fear, a dread of something that he himself did not understand. He was more conscious of this fear when he was alone, and he had, therefore, thrown himself eagerly into community life.

It was about that time he became conscious of Carol.

He had known Carol all his life. They had gone to school together. She was two years younger than he was, a gawky, sweet-tempered child, with a brace on her teeth and a shy manner. Their parents were friends, and Carol spent a lot of time in the Knox household.

In the year of taking his finals, Llewellyn came home and saw Carol with new eyes. The brace was gone, and so was the gawkiness. Instead there was a pretty coquettish young girl, whom all the boys were anxious to date up.

Girls had so far not impinged much on Llewellyn's life. He had worked too hard, and was, moreover, emotionally undeveloped. But now the manhood in him suddenly came to life. He started taking trouble with his appearance, spent money he could ill afford on new ties, and bought boxes of candy to present to Carol. His mother smiled and sighed, as mothers do, at the signs that her son had entered on maturity! The time had come when she must lose him to another woman. Too early to think of marriage as yet, but if it had to come, Carol would be a satisfactory choice. Good stock, carefully brought up, a sweet-tempered girl, and healthy—better than some strange girl from the city whom she did not know. 'But not good enough for my son,' said her mother's heart, and then she smiled at herself, guessing that that was what all mothers had felt since time immemorial! She spoke hesitantly to Angus of the matter.

"Early days yet," said Angus. "The lad has his way to make. But he might do worse. She's a good lass, though maybe not overloaded with brains."

Carol was both pretty and popular, and enjoyed her popularity. She had plenty of dates, but she made it fairly clear that Llewellyn was the favourite. She talked to him sometimes in a serious way about his future. Though she did not show it, she was slightly disconcerted by his vagueness and what seemed to her his lack of ambition.

"Why, Lew, surely you've got *some* definite plans for when you've qualified?"

"Oh! I shall get a job all right. Plenty of openings."

"But don't you have to specialise nowadays?"

"If one has any particular bent. I haven't."

"But, Llewellyn Knox, you want to get on, don't you?"

"Get on—where?" His smile was slightly teasing.

"Well—get *somewhere.*"

"But that is life, isn't it, Carol? From here to here." His finger traced a line on the sand. "Birth, growth, school, career, marriage, children, home, hard work, retirement, old age, death. From the frontier of this country to the frontier of the next."

"That's not what I mean at all, Lew, and you know it. I mean getting *somewhere,* making a name for yourself, making good, getting right to the top, so that everyone's proud of you."

"I wonder if all that makes any difference," he said abstractedly.

"I'll say it makes a difference!"

"It's *how* you go through your journey that matters, I think, not where it takes you."

"I never heard such nonsense. Don't you *want* to be a success?"

"I don't know. I don't think so."

Carol was a long way away from him suddenly. He was alone, quite alone, and he was conscious of fear. A shrinking, a terrible shrinking. "Not me—someone else." He almost said the words aloud.

"Lew! Llewellyn!" Carol's voice came thinly to him from a long way away, coming towards him through the wilderness. "What's the matter? You look downright queer."

He was back again, back with Carol, who was staring at him with a perplexed, frightened expression. He was conscious of a rush of tenderness towards her. She had saved him, called him back from that barren place. He took her hand.

"You're so sweet." He drew her towards him, kissed her gently, almost shyly. Her lips responded to his.

He thought: 'I can tell her now . . . that I love her . . . that when I'm qualified we can get engaged. I'll ask her to wait for me. Once I've got Carol, I'll be safe.'

But the words remained unspoken. He felt something that was almost like a physical hand on his breast, pushing him back, a hand that forbade. The reality of it alarmed him. He got up.

"Some day, Carol," he said, "some day I—I've got to talk to you."

She looked up at him and laughed, satisfied. She was not particularly anxious for him to come to the point. Things were best left as they were. She enjoyed in an innocent happy fashion her own young girl's hour of triumph, courted by the young males. Some day she and Llewellyn would marry. She had felt the emotion behind his kiss. She was quite sure of him.

As for his queer lack of ambition, that did not really worry her. Women in this country were confident of their power over men. It was women who planned and urged on their men to achieve; women, and the children that were their principal weapons. She and Llewellyn would want the best for their children, and that would be a spur to urge Llewellyn on.

As for Llewellyn, he walked home in a serious state of perturbation. What a very odd experience that had been. Full of recent lectures on psychology, he analysed himself with misgiving. A resistance to sex perhaps? Why had he set up this resistance? He ate his supper staring at his mother, and wondering uneasily if he had an Oedipus Complex.

Nevertheless, it was to her he came for reassurance before he went back to college.

He said abruptly:

"You like Carol, don't you?"

Here it comes, she thought with a pang, but she said steadfastly:

"She's a sweet girl. Both your father and I like her well."

"I wanted to tell her—the other day—"

"That you loved her?"

"Yes. I wanted to ask her to wait for me."

"No need of that, if she loves you, bach."

"But I couldn't say it, the words wouldn't come."

She smiled. "Don't let that worry you. Men are mostly tongue-tied at these times. There was your father sitting and glowering at me, day after day, more as though he hated me than loved me, and not able to get a word out but 'How are you?' and 'It's a fine day.' "

Llewellyn said sombrely: "It was more than that. It was like a hand shoving me back. It was as though I was —*forbidden*."

She felt then the urgency and force of his trouble. She said slowly:

"It may be that she's not the real girl for you. Oh—" she stifled his protest. "It's hard to tell when you're young and the blood rises. But there's something in you—the true self, maybe—that knows what should and shouldn't be, and that saves you from yourself, and the impulse that isn't the true one."

"Something in oneself . . ." He dwelt on that.

He looked at her with sudden desperate eyes.

"I don't know really—anything about myself."

2

Back at college, he filled up every moment, either with work or in the company of friends. Fear faded away from him. He felt self-assured once more. He read abstruse dissertations on adolescent sex manifestations, and explained himself to himself satisfactorily.

He graduated with distinction, and that, too, encouraged him to have confidence in himself. He returned home with his mind made up, and his future clear ahead. He would ask Carol to marry him, and discuss with her the various possibilities open to him now that he was qualified. He felt an enormous relief now that his life unfolded before him in so clear a sequence. Work that was congenial and which he felt himself competent to do well, and a girl he loved with whom to make a home and have children.

Arrived at home, he threw himself into all the local festivities. He went about in a crowd, but within that crowd he and Carol paired off and were accepted as a pair. He was seldom, if ever, alone, and when he went to bed at night he slept and dreamed of Carol. They were erotic dreams and he welcomed them as such. Everything was normal, everything was fine, everything was as it should be.

Confident in this belief, he was startled when his father said to him one day:

"What's wrong, lad?"

"Wrong?" He stared.

"You're not yourself."

"But I am! I've never felt so fit!"

"You're well enough physically, maybe."

Llewellyn stared at his father. The gaunt, aloof old man, with his deep-set burning eyes, nodded his head slowly.

"There are times," he said, "when a man needs to be alone."

He said no more, turning away, as Llewellyn felt once more that swift illogical fear spring up. He *didn't* want to be alone—it was the last thing he wanted. He couldn't, he *mustn't* be alone.

Three days later he came to his father and said:

"I'm going camping in the mountains. By myself."

Angus nodded. "Ay."

His eyes, the eyes of a mystic, looked at his son with comprehension.

Llewellyn thought: 'I've inherited something from him —something that *he* knows about, and I don't know about yet.'

3

He had been alone here, in the desert, for nearly three weeks. Curious things had been happening to him. From the very first, however, he had found solitude quite acceptable. He wondered why he had fought against the idea of it so long.

To begin with, he had thought a great deal about himself and his future and Carol. It had all unrolled itself quite clearly and logically, and it was not for some time that he realised that he was looking at his life from *outside*, as a spectator and not a participator. That was because none of that mapped-out planned existence was real. It was logical and coherent, but in fact it did not exist. He loved Carol, he desired her, but he would not marry her. He had something else to do. As yet he did not know what. After he had acknowledged that fact, there came another phase—a phase he could only describe as one of emptiness, great echoing emptiness. He was nothing, and contained nothing. There was no longer any fear. By accepting emptiness, he had cast out fear.

During this phase, he ate and drank hardly anything. Sometimes he was, he thought, slightly light-headed.

Like a mirage in front of him, scenes and people appeared.

Once or twice he saw a face very clearly. It was a woman's face, and it roused in him an extraordinary excitement. It had fragile, very beautiful bones, with hollowed temples, and dark hair springing back from the temples, and deep, almost tragic eyes. Behind her he saw, once, a background of flames, and another time the shadowy outline of what looked like a church. This time, he saw suddenly that she was only a child. Each time he was conscious of suffering. He thought: 'If I could only help . . .' But at the same time he knew that there was no help possible, and that the very idea was wrong and false.

Another vision was of a gigantic office desk in pale shining wood, and behind it a man with a heavy jowl and small, alert, blue eyes. The man leant forward as though about to speak, and to do so emphasised what he was about to say by picking up a small ruler and gesticulating with it.

Then again he saw the corner of a room at a curious angle. Near it was a window, and through the window the outlines of a pine tree with snow on it. Between him and the window, a face obtruded, looking down on him—a round, pink-faced man with glasses, but before Llewellyn could see him really clearly, he, too, faded away.

All these visions must, Llewellyn thought, be the figments of his own imagination. There seemed so little sense or meaning to them, and they were all faces and surroundings that he had never known.

But soon there were no more pictorial images. The emptiness of which he was so conscious was no longer vast and all-encompassing. The emptiness drew together, it acquired meaning and purpose. He was no longer adrift in it. Instead, he held it within himself.

Then he knew something more. He was waiting.

4

The dust-storm came suddenly—one of those unheralded storms that arose in this mountainous desert region. It came whirling and shrieking in clouds of red dust. It was like a live thing. It ended as suddenly as it had begun. After it, the silence was very noticeable.

All Llewellyn's camping gear had been swept away by the wind, his tent carried flapping and whirling like a mad thing down the valley. He had nothing now. He was quite alone in a world suddenly peaceful and as though made anew.

He knew now that something he had always known would happen was about to happen. He knew fear again, but not the fear he had felt before, that had been the fear of resistance. This time he was ready to accept—there was emptiness within him, swept and garnished, ready to receive a Presence. He was afraid only because in all humility he knew what a small and insignificant entity he was.

It was not easy to explain to Wilding what came next.

"Because, you see, there aren't any words for it. But I'm quite clear as to *what* it was. It was the recognition of God. I can express it best by saying that it was as though a blind man who believed in the sun from literary evidence, and who had felt its warmth on his hand, was suddenly to open his eyes and *see* it.

"I had *believed* in God, but now I *knew*. It was direct personal knowledge, quite indescribable. And a most terrifying experience for any human being. I understood then why, in God's approach to man, He has to incarnate Himself in human flesh.

"Afterwards—it only lasted a few seconds of time—I turned around and went home. It took me two or three days, and I was very weak and exhausted when I staggered in."

He was silent for a moment or two.

"My mother was dreadfully worried over me! She couldn't make it all out. My father, I think, had an inkling. He knew, at least, that I had had some vast experience. I told my mother that I had had curious visions that I couldn't explain, and she said: 'They have the "sight" in your father's family. His grandmother had it, and one of his sisters.'

"After a few days of rest and feeding up, I was strong again. When people talked of my future, I was silent. I knew that all that would be settled for me. I had only to accept—I had accepted—but *what* it was I had accepted, I didn't yet know.

"A week later, there was a big prayer meeting held in the neighbourhood. A kind of Revivalist Mission is how I think you describe it. My mother wanted to go, and my father was willing, though not much interested. I went with them."

Looking at Wilding, Llewellyn smiled.

"It wasn't the sort of thing *you* would have cared for—crude, rather melodramatic. It didn't move me. I was a little disappointed that that was so. Various people got up to testify. Then the command came to me, clear and quite unmistakable.

"I got up. I remember the faces turning to me.

"I didn't know what I was going to say. I didn't think—or expound my own beliefs. The words were there in my head. Sometimes they got ahead of me, I had to speak faster to catch up, to say them before I lost them. I can't describe to you what it was like—if I said it was like flame and like honey, would you understand at all? The flame seared me, but the sweetness of the honey was there too, the sweetness of obedience. It is both a terrible and a lovely thing to be the messenger of God."

"Terrible as an army with banners," murmured Wilding.

"Yes. The psalmist knew what he was talking about."

"And—afterwards?"

Llewellyn Knox spread out his hands.

"Exhaustion, utter and complete exhaustion. I must have spoken, I suppose, for about three-quarters of an hour. When I got home, I sat by the fire shivering, too dead to lift a hand or to speak. My mother understood. She said: 'It is like my father was, after the Eisteddfod.' She gave me hot soup and put hot-water-bottles in my bed."

Wilding murmured: "You had all the necessary heredity. The mystic from the Scottish side, and the poetic and creative from the Welsh—the voice, too. And it's a true creative picture—the fear, the frustration, the emptiness, and then the sudden up-rush of power, and after it, the weariness."

He was silent for a moment, and then asked:

"Won't you go on with the story?"

"There's not so much more to tell. I went and saw Carol the next day. I told her I wasn't going to be a doctor after all, that I was going to be a preacher of some kind. I told her that I had hoped to marry her, but that now I had to give up that hope. She didn't understand. She said: 'A doctor can do just as much good as a preacher can do.' And I said it wasn't a question of doing good. It was a command, and I had to obey it. And she said it was nonsense saying I couldn't get married. I wasn't a Roman Catholic, was I? And I said: 'Everything I am, and have, has to be God's.' But of course she couldn't see that—how could she, poor child? It wasn't in her vocabulary. I went home and told my mother, and asked her to be good to Carol, and begged her to understand. She said: 'I understand well enough. You'll have nothing left over to give a woman,' and then she broke down and cried, and said: 'I knew—I always knew—there was *something*. You were different from the others. Ah, but it's hard on the wives and mothers.'

"She said: 'If I lost you to a woman, that's the way of life, and there would have been your children for me to hold on my knee. But this way, you'll be gone from me entirely.'

"I assured her that wasn't true, but all the time we both knew that it was in essence. Human ties—they all had to go."

Wilding moved restlessly.

"You must forgive me, but I can't subscribe to that, as a way of life. Human affection, human sympathy, service to humanity—"

"But it isn't a way of life that I am talking about! I am talking of the man singled out, the man who is something more than his fellows, and who is also very much less—that is the thing he must never forget, how infinitely less than they he is, and must be."

"There I can't follow you."

Llewellyn spoke softly, more to himself than to his listener.

"That, of course, is the danger—that one will forget. That, I see now, is where God showed mercy to me. I was saved in time."

Chapter six

1

Wilding looked faintly puzzled by Llewellyn's last words.

He said with a faint trace of embarrassment: "It's good of you to have told me all you have. Please believe that it wasn't just vulgar curiosity on my part."

"I know that. You have a real interest in your fellow-man."

"And you are an unusual specimen. I've read in various periodicals accounts of your career. But it wasn't those things that interested me. Those details are merely factual."

Llewellyn nodded. His mind was still occupied with the past. He was remembering the day when the elevator had swept him up to the thirty-fifth floor of a high building. The reception-room, the tall, elegant blonde who had received him, the square-shouldered, thick-set young man, to whom she had handed him over, and the final sanctuary; the inner office of the magnate. The gleaming pale surface of the vast desk, and the man who rose from behind the desk to proffer a hand and utter a welcome. The big jowl, the small, piercing blue eyes. Just as he had seen them that day in the desert.

". . . certainly glad to make your acquaintance, Mr. Knox. As I see it, the country is ripe for a great return to God . . . got to be put over in a big way . . . to get results we've got to spend money . . . been to two of your meetings . . . I certainly was impressed . . . you'd got them right with you, eating up every word . . . it was great . . . great!"

God and Big Business. Did they seem incongruous together? And yet, why should they? If business acumen was one of God's gifts to man, why should it not be used in his service?

He, Llewellyn, had had no doubts or qualms, for this room and this man had already been shown to him. It was part of the pattern, *his* pattern. Was there sincerity here, a simple sincerity that might seem as grotesque as the early carvings on a font? Or was it the mere grasping of a business opportunity? The realisation that God might be made to pay?

Llewellyn had never known, had not, indeed, troubled himself even to wonder. It was part of his pattern. He was a messenger, nothing more, a man under obedience.

Fifteen years . . . From the small open-air meetings of the beginning, to lecture-rooms, to halls, to vast stadiums.

Faces, blurred gigantic masses of faces, receding into the distance, rising up in serried rows. Waiting, hungering . . .

And his part? Always the same.

The coldness, the recoil of fear, the emptiness, the waiting.

And then Dr. Llewellyn Knox rises to his feet and . . . the words come, rushing through his mind, emerging through his lips. . . . Not his words, never his words. But the glory, the ecstasy of speaking them, that was his.

(That, of course, was where the danger had lain. Strange that he should not have realised that until now.)

And then the aftermath, the fawning women, the hearty men, his own sense of semi-collapse, of deadly nausea, the hospitality, the adulation, the hysteria.

And he himself, responding as best he could, no longer the messenger of God, but the inadequate human being, something far less than those who looked at him with their foolish worshipping gaze. For virtue had gone out of him, he was drained of all that gives a man human dignity, a sick exhausted creature, filled with despair, black, empty, hollow despair.

"Poor Dr. Knox," they said, "he looks so tired."

Tired. More and more tired . . .

He had been a strong man physically, but not strong enough to outlast fifteen years. Nausea, giddiness, a fluttering heart, a difficulty in drawing breath, black-outs, fainting spells—quite simply, a worn-out body.

And so to the sanatorium in the mountains. Lying there motionless, staring out through the window at the dark shape of the pine tree cutting the line of the sky, and the round, pink face bending over him, the eyes behind the thick glasses, owlish in their solemnity.

"It will be a long business; you'll have to be patient."

"Yes, doctor?"

"You've a strong constitution fortunately, but you've strained it unmercifully. Heart, lungs—every organ in your body has been affected."

"Are you breaking it to me that I'm going to die?"

He had asked the question with only mild curiosity.

"Certainly not. We'll get you right again. As I say, it will be a long business, but you'll go out of here a fit man. Only—"

The doctor hesitated.

"Only what?"

"You must understand this, Dr. Knox. You'll have to lead a quiet life in future. There must be no more public life. Your heart won't stand it. No platforms, no exertion, no speeches."

"After a rest—"

"No, Dr. Knox, however long you rest, my verdict will be the same."

"I see." He thought about it. "I see. Worn out?"

"Just that."

Worn out. Used by God for His purpose, but the instrument, being human and frail, had not lasted long. His usefulness was over. Used, discarded, thrown away.

And what next?

That was the question? What next?

Because, after all, who was he, Llewellyn Knox?

He would have to find out.

2

Wilding's voice came in, pat upon his thoughts.

"Is it in order for me to ask you what your future plans are?"

"I have no plans."

"Really? You hope, perhaps, to go back—"

Llewellyn interrupted, a slight harshness in his voice.

"There is no going back."

"Some modified form of activity?"

"No. It's a clean break—has to be."

"They told you that?"

"Not in so many words. Public life is out, was what they stressed. No more platform. That means finish."

"A quiet living somewhere? Living is not your term, I know, but I mean minister to some church?"

"I was an Evangelist, Sir Richard. That's a very different thing."

"I'm sorry. I think I understand. You've got to start an entirely new life."

"Yes, a private life, as a man."

"And that confuses and alarms you?"

Llewellyn shook his head.

"Nothing like that. I see, I've seen it plainly in the weeks I've been here, that I've escaped a great danger."

"What danger?"

"Man cannot be trusted with power. It rots him—from within. How much longer could I have gone on without the taint creeping in? I suspect that already it had begun to work. Those moments when I spoke to those vast crowds of people—wasn't I beginning to assume that it was *I* who was speaking, *I* who was giving them a message, I who knew just what they should or should not do, I who was no longer just God's messenger, but God's representative? You see? Promoted to Vizier, exalted, a man set above other men!" He added quietly: "God in His goodness has seen fit to save me from that."

"Then your faith has not been diminished by what has happened to you?"

Llewellyn laughed.

"Faith? That seems an odd word to me. Do we believe in the sun, the moon, the chair we sit in, the ground we walk upon? If one has knowledge, what need of belief? And do disabuse your mind of the idea that I've suffered some kind of tragedy. I haven't, I've pursued my appointed course—am still pursuing it. It was right for me to come here—to the island; it will be right for me to leave it when the time comes."

"You mean you will get another—what did you call it?—command?"

"Oh no, nothing so definite. But little by little a certain course of action will appear not only to be desirable, but inevitable. Then I shall go ahead and act. Things will clarify themselves in my mind. I shall know where I have to go and what I have to do."

"As easy as that?"

"I think so—yes. If I can explain it, it's a question of being in *harmony*. A wrong course of action—and by wrong I don't mean wrong in the sense of evil, but of being mistaken—is felt at once: it's like falling out of step if you're dancing, or singing a false note— it jars." Moved by a sudden memory, he said: "If I was a woman, I dare say it would feel like getting a stitch wrong when you were knitting."

"What about women? Will you, perhaps, go back home? Find your early love?"

"The sentimental ending? Hardly. Besides," he smiled, "Carol has been married for many years now. She has three children, and her husband is going ahead in real estate in a big way. Carol and I were never meant for each other. It was a boy and girl affair that never went deep."

"Has there been no other woman in all these years?"

"No, thank God. If there had been, if I had met her then—"

He left the sentence unfinished, puzzling Wilding a little by so doing. Wilding could have no clue to the picture that sprang up before Llewellyn's mental vision— the wings of dark hair, the frail delicate temple-bones, the tragic eyes.

Some day, Llewellyn knew, he would meet her. She was as real as the office desk and the sanatorium had been. She existed. If he had met her during the time of his dedication he would have been forced to give her up. It would have been required of him. Could he have done it? He doubted himself. His dark lady was no Carol, no light affair born of the spring-time and a young man's quickened senses. But that sacrifice had not been demanded of him. Now he was free. When they met . . . He had no doubt that they would meet. Under what circumstances, in what place, at what moment of time—all that was unknown. A stone font in a church, tongues of fire, those were the only indications he had. Yet he had the feeling that he was coming very near, that it would not be long now.

The abruptness with which the door between the bookcases opened, startled him. Wilding turned his head, rose to his feet with a gesture of surprise.

"Darling, I didn't expect—"

She was not wearing the Spanish shawl, or the highnecked black dress. She had on something diaphanous and floating in pale mauve, and it was the colour, perhaps, that made Llewellyn feel that she brought with her the old-fashioned scent of lavender. She stopped when she saw him; her eyes, wide and slightly glazed, stared at him, expressing such a complete lack of emotion that it was almost shocking.

"Dearest, is your head better? This is Dr. Knox. My wife."

Llewellyn came forward, took her limp hand, said formally: "I'm very pleased to make your acquaintance, Lady Wilding."

The wide stare became human; it showed, very faintly, relief. She sat in the chair that Wilding pushed forward for her and began talking rapidly, with a staccato effect.

"So you're Dr. Knox? I've read about you, of course. How odd that you should come here—to the island. Why did you? I mean, what made you? People don't usually, do they, Richard?" She half turned her head, hurried on, inconsequently:

"I mean they don't stay in the island. They come in on boats, and go out again. Where? I've often wondered. They buy fruit and those silly little dolls and the straw hats they make here, and then they go back with them to the boat, and the boat sails away. Where do they go back to? Manchester? Liverpool? Chichester, perhaps, and wear a plaited straw hat to church in the cathedral. That would be funny. Things are funny. People say: 'I don't know whether I'm going or coming.' My old nurse used to say it. But it's true, isn't it? It's life. Is one going or coming? I don't know."

She shook her head and suddenly laughed. She swayed a little as she sat. Llewellyn thought: 'In a minute or two, she'll pass out. Does he know, I wonder?'

But a quick sideways glance at Wilding decided that for him. Wilding, that experienced man of the world, had no idea. He was leaning over his wife, his face alight with love and anxiety.

"Darling, you're feverish. You shouldn't have got up."

"I felt better—all those pills I took; it's killed the pain, but it's made me dopey." She gave a slight, uncertain laugh, her hands pushed the pale, shining hair back from her forehead. "Don't fuss about me, Richard. Give Dr. Knox a drink."

"What about you? A spot of brandy? It would do you good."

She made a quick grimace:

"No, just lime and soda for me."

She thanked him with a smile as he brought her glass to her.

"You'll never die of drink," he said.

For a moment her smile stiffened.

She said:

"Who knows?"

"I know. Knox, what about you? Soft drink? Whisky?"

"Brandy and soda, if I may."

Her eyes were on the glass as he held it.

She said suddenly: "We could go away. Shall we go away, Richard?"

"Away from the villa? From the island?"

"That's what I meant."

Wilding poured his own whisky, came back to stand behind her chair.

"We'll go anywhere you please, dearest. Anywhere and at any time. To-night if you like."

She sighed, a long, deep sigh.

"You're so—good to me. Of course I don't want to leave here. Anyway, how could you? You've got the estate to run. You're making headway at last."

"Yes, but that doesn't really matter. You come first."

"I might go away—by myself—just for a little."

"No, we'll go together. I want you to feel looked after, someone beside you—always."

"You think I need a keeper?" She began to laugh. It was slightly uncontrolled laughter. She stopped suddenly, hand to her mouth.

"I want you to feel—always—that I'm there," said Wilding.

"Oh, I do feel it—I do."

"We'll go to Italy. Or to England, if you like. Perhaps you're home-sick for England."

"No," she said. "We won't go anywhere. We'll stay here. It would be the same wherever we went. Always the same."

She slumped a little in her chair. Her eyes stared sombrely ahead of her. Then suddenly she looked up over her shoulder, up into Wilding's puzzled, worried face.

"Dear Richard," she said. "You are so wonderful to me. So patient always."

He said softly: "So long as you understand that to me nothing matters but you."

"I know that—oh, I do know it."

He went on:

"I hoped that you would be happy here, but I do realise that there's very little—distraction."

"There's Dr. Knox," she said.

Her head turned swiftly towards the guest, and a sudden gay, impish smile flashed at him. He thought: 'What a gay, what an enchanting creature she could be— has been.'

She went on: "And as for the island and the villa, it's an earthly paradise. You said so once, and I believed you, and it's true. It *is* an earthly paradise."

"Ah!"

"But I can't quite take it. Don't you think, Dr. Knox" —the slight staccato tempo returned—"that one has to be rather a strong character to stand up to paradise? Like those old Primitives, the blessed sitting in a row under the trees, wearing crowns—I always thought the crowns looked so heavy—casting down their golden crowns before the glassy sea—that's a hymn, isn't it? Perhaps God let them cast down the crowns because of the weight. It's heavy to wear a crown all the time. One can have too much of everything, can't one? I think—" She got up, stumbled a little. "I think, perhaps, I'll go back to bed. I think you're right, Richard, perhaps I am feverish. But crowns are heavy. Being here is like a dream come true, only I'm not in the dream any more. I ought to be some-where else, but I don't know where. If only—"

She crumpled very suddenly, and Llewellyn, who had been waiting for it, caught her in time, relinquishing her a moment later to Wilding.

"Better get her back to her bed," he advised crisply.

"Yes, yes. And then I'll telephone to the doctor."

"She'll sleep it off," said Llewellyn.

Richard Wilding looked at him doubtfully.

Llewellyn said: "Let me help you."

The two men carried the unconscious girl through the door by which she had entered the room. A short way along a corridor brought them to the open door of a bed-room. They laid her gently on the big carved wooden bed, with its hangings of rich dark brocade. Wilding went out into the corridor and called: "Maria—Maria."

Llewellyn looked swiftly round the room.

He went through a curtained alcove into a bathroom, looked into the glass-panelled cupboard there, then came back to the bedroom.

Wilding was calling again: "Maria," impatiently.

Llewellyn moved over to the dressing-table.

A moment or two later Wilding came into the room, followed by a short, dark woman. The latter moved quickly across the room to the bed and uttered an ex-clamation as she bent over the recumbent girl.

Wilding said curtly:

"See to your mistress. I will ring up the doctor."

"It is not necessary, señor. I know what to do. By to-morrow morning she will be herself again."

Wilding, shaking his head, left the room reluctantly.

Llewellyn followed him, but paused in the doorway.

He said: "Where does she keep it?"

The woman looked at him; her eyelids flickered.

Then, almost involuntarily, her gaze shifted to the wall behind his head. He turned. A small picture hung there, a landscape in the manner of Corot. Llewellyn raised it from its nail. Behind it was a small wall safe of the old-fashioned type, where women used to keep their jewels, but which would hold little protection against a modern cracksman. The key was in the lock. Llewellyn pulled it gently open and glanced inside. He nodded and closed it again. His eyes met those of Maria in perfect comprehension.

He went out of the room and joined Wilding, who was just replacing the telephone on its cradle.

"The doctor is out, at a confinement, I understand."

"I think," said Llewellyn, choosing his words carefully, "that Maria knows what to do. She has, I think, seen Lady Wilding like this before."

"Yes . . . yes . . . Perhaps you are right. She is very devoted to my wife."

"I saw that."

"Everybody loves her. She inspires love—love, and the wish to protect. All these people here have a great feeling for beauty, and especially for beauty in distress."

"And yet they are, in their way, greater realists than the Anglo-Saxon will ever be."

"Possibly."

"They don't shirk facts."

"Do we?"

"Very often. That is a beautiful room of your wife's. Do you know what struck me about it? There was no smell of perfume such as many women delight in. Instead, there was only the fragrance of lavender and eau-de-Cologne."

Richard Wilding nodded.

"I know. I have come to associate lavender with Shirley. It brings back to me my days as a boy, the smell of lavender in my mother's linen-cupboard. The fine white linen, and the little bags of lavender that she made and put there, clean, pure, all the freshness of spring. Simple country things."

He sighed and looked up to see his guest regarding him with a look he could not understand.

"I must go," said Llewellyn, holding out his hand.

Chapter seven

"So you still come here?"

Knox delayed his question until the waiter had gone away.

Lady Wilding was silent for a moment. To-night she was not staring out at the harbour. Instead she was looking down into her glass. It held a rich golden liquid.

"Orange juice," she said.

"I see. A gesture."

"Yes. It helps—to make a gesture."

"Oh, undoubtedly."

She said: "Did you tell him that you had seen me here?"

"No."

"Why not?"

"It would have caused him pain. It would have caused you pain. And he didn't ask me."

"If he had asked you, would you have told him?"

"Yes."

"Why?"

"Because the simpler one is over things, the better." She sighed.

"I wonder if you understand at all?"

"I don't know."

"You do see that I can't hurt him? You do see how good he is? How he believes in me? How he thinks only of me?"

"Oh yes. I see all that. He wants to stand between you and all sorrow, all evil."

"But that's too much."

"Yes, it's too much."

"One gets into things. And then, one can't get out. One pretends—day after day one pretends. And then one gets tired, one wants to shout: 'Stop loving me, stop looking after me, stop worrying about me, stop caring and watching.' " She clenched both hands. "I *want* to be happy with Richard. I want to! Why can't I? Why must I sicken of it all?"

"Stay me with flagons, comfort me with apples, for I am sick of love."

"Yes, just that. It's *me*. It's my fault."

"Why did you marry him?"

"Oh, that!" Her eyes widened. "That's simple. I fell in love with him."

"I see."

"It was, I suppose, a kind of infatuation. He has great charm, and he's sexually attractive. Do you understand?"

"Yes, I understand."

"And he was romantically attractive too. A dear old man, who's known me all my life, warned me. He said to me: 'Have an affair with Richard, but don't marry him.' He was quite right. You see, I was very unhappy, and Richard came along. I—day-dreamed. Love and Richard and an island and moonlight. It helped, and it didn't hurt anybody. Now I've got the dream—but I'm not the me I was in the dream. I'm only the me who dreamed it—and that's no good."

She looked across the table, straight into his eyes.

"Can I ever become the me of the dream? I'd like to."

"Not if it was never the real you."

"I could go away—but where? Not back into the past

because that's all gone, broken up. I'd have to start again, I don't know how or where. And, anyway, I couldn't hurt Richard. He's already been hurt too much."

"Has he?"

"Yes, that woman he married. She was just a natural tart. Very attractive and quite good-natured, but completely amoral. He didn't see her like that."

"He wouldn't."

"And she let him down—badly—and he was terribly cut up about it. He blamed himself, thought he'd failed her in some way. He's no blame for her, you know, only pity."

"He has too much pity."

"Can one have too much pity?"

"Yes, it makes you unable to see straight."

"Besides," he added, "it's an insult."

"What *do* you mean?"

"It implies just what the Pharisee's prayer implied. 'Lord, I thank Thee I am not as this man.'"

"Aren't *you* ever sorry for anyone?"

"Yes. I'm human. But I'm afraid of it."

"What harm could it do?"

"It might lead to action."

"Would that be wrong?"

"It might have very bad results."

"For you?"

"No, no, not for me. For the other person."

"Then what should one do if one's sorry for a person?"

"Leave them where they belong—in God's hands."

"That sounds terribly implacable—and harsh."

"It's not nearly so dangerous as yielding to facile pity."

She leaned towards him.

"Tell me, are you sorry for me—at all?"

"I am trying not to be."

"Why not?"

"In case I should help you to feel sorry for yourself."

"You don't think I am—sorry for myself?"

"Are you?"

"No," she said slowly. "Not really. I've got all—mixed up somehow, and that must be my own fault."

"It usually is, but in your case it may not be."

"Tell me—you're wise, you go about preaching to people—what ought I to do?"

"You know."

She looked at him and suddenly, unexpectedly, she laughed. It was a gay, gallant laugh.

"Yes," she said. "I know. Quite well. *Fight*."

part 4

*As It Was in the
Beginning-1956*

Chapter one

Llewellyn looked up at the building before he entered it.

It was drab like the street in which it stood. Here, in this quarter of London, war damage and general decay still reigned. The effect was depressing. Llewellyn himself felt depressed. The errand which he had come to perform was a painful one. He did not exactly shrink from it, but he was aware that he would be glad when he had discharged it to the best of his ability.

He sighed, squared his shoulders, and went up a short flight of steps and through a swing door.

The inside of the building was busy, but busy in an orderly and controlled fashion. Hurrying but disciplined feet sped along the corridors. A young woman in a dull blue uniform paused beside him.

"What can I do for you?"

"I wish to see Miss Franklin."

"I'm sorry. Miss Franklin can't see anyone this morning. I will take you to the secretary's office."

He insisted gently on seeing Miss Franklin.

"It is important," he said, and added: "If you will please give her this letter."

The young woman took him into a minute waiting-room and sped away. Five minutes later a round woman with a kindly face and an eager manner came to him.

"I'm Miss Harrison, Miss Franklin's secretary. I'm afraid you will have to wait a few minutes. Miss Franklin is with one of the children who is just coming out of the anaesthetic after an operation."

Llewellyn thanked her and began to ask questions. She brightened at once, and talked eagerly about the Worley Foundation for Sub-Normal Children.

"It's quite an old foundation, you know. Dates back to 1840: Nathaniel Worley, our founder, was a mill-owner." Her voice ran on. "So unfortunate—the funds dwindled, investments brought in so much less . . . and rising costs . . . of course there were faults of administration. But since Miss Franklin has been superintendent . . ."

Her face lighted up, the speed of her words increased.

Miss Franklin was clearly the sun in her heaven. Miss Franklin had cleaned the Augean stables, Miss Franklin had reorganised this and that, Miss Franklin had battled with authority and won, and now, equally clearly, Miss Franklin reigned supreme, and all was for the best in the best of possible worlds. Llewellyn wondered why women's enthusiasms for other women always sounded so pitifully crude. He doubted if he should like the efficient Miss Franklin. She was, he thought, of the order of Queen Bees. Other women buzzed round them, and they waxed and throve on the power thus accorded to them.

Then at last he was taken upstairs and along a corridor, and Miss Harrison knocked at a door and stood aside, and motioned to him to go in to what was evidently the Holy of Holies—Miss Franklin's private office.

She was sitting behind a desk, and she looked frail and very tired.

He stared at her in awe and amazement as she got up and came towards him.

He said, just under his breath: *"You . . . "*

A faint, puzzled frown came between her brows, those delicately marked brows that he knew so well. It was the same face—pale, delicate, the wide sad mouth, the unusual setting of the dark eyes, the hair that sprang back from the temples, triumphantly, like wings. A tragic face, he thought, yet that generous mouth was made for laughter, that severe, proud face might be transformed by tenderness.

She said gently: "Dr. Llewellyn? My brother-in-law wrote to me that you would be coming. It's very good of you."

"I'm afraid the news of your sister's death must have been a great shock to you."

"Oh, it was. She was so young."

Her voice faltered for one moment, but she had herself well under control. He thought to himself: "She is disciplined, has disciplined herself."

There was something nun-like about her clothes. She wore plain black with a little white at the throat.

She said quietly:

"I wish it could have been I who died—not her. But perhaps one always wishes that."

"Not always. Only—if one cares very much—or if one's own life has some quality of the unbearable about it."

The dark eyes opened wider. She looked at him questioningly, she said:

"You're really Llewellyn Knox, aren't you?"

"I was. I call myself Dr. Murray Llewellyn. It saves the endless repetition of condolences, makes it less embarrassing for other people and for me."

"I've seen pictures of you in the papers, but I don't think I would have recognised you."

"No. Most people don't, now. There are other faces in the news—and perhaps, too, I've shrunk."

"Shrunk?"

He smiled.

"Not physically, but in importance."

He went on:

"You know that I've brought your sister's small personal possessions. Your brother-in-law thought you would like to have them. They are at my hotel. Perhaps you will dine with me there, or if you prefer, I will deliver them to you here?"

"I shall be glad to have them. I want to hear all you can tell me about—about Shirley. It is so long since I saw her last. Nearly three years. I still can't believe—that she's *dead*."

"I know how you feel."

"I want to hear all you can tell me about her, but—but—don't say consoling things to me. You still believe in God, I suppose. Well, I don't! I'm sorry if that seems a crude thing to say, but you'd better understand what I feel. If there *is* a God, He is cruel and unjust."

"Because He let your sister die?"

"There's no need to discuss it. Please don't talk religion to me. Tell me about Shirley. Even now I don't understand how the accident happened."

"She was crossing the street and a heavy lorry knocked her down and ran over her. She was killed instantly. She did not suffer any pain."

"That's what Richard wrote me. But I thought—perhaps he was trying to be kind, to spare me. He is like that."

"Yes, he is like that. But I am not. You can take it as the truth that your sister was killed outright, and did not suffer."

"How did it happen?"

"It was late at night. Your sister had been sitting in one of the open-air cafés facing the harbour. She left the café, crossed the road without looking, and the lorry came round the corner and caught her."

"Was she alone?"

"Quite alone."

"But where was Richard? Why wasn't he with her? It seems so extraordinary. I shouldn't have thought Richard would have let her go off by herself at night to a café. I should have thought he would have looked after her, taken care of her."

"You mustn't blame him. He adored her. He watched over her in every way possible. On this occasion he didn't know she had left the house."

Her face softened.

"I see. I've been unjust."

She pressed her hands together.

"It's so cruel, so unfair, so *meaningless*. After all Shirley had been through. To have only three years of happiness."

He did not answer at once, just sat watching her.

"Forgive me, you loved your sister very much?"

"More than anyone in the world."

"And yet, for three years you never saw her. They invited you, repeatedly, but you never came?"

"It was difficult to leave my work here, to find someone to replace me."

"That, perhaps; but it could have been managed. Why didn't you want to go?"

"I did. I did!"

"But you had some reason for not going?"

"I've told you. My work here——"

"Do you love your work so much?"

"Love it? No." She seemed surprised. "But it's worthwhile work. It answers a need. These children were in a category that was not catered for. I think——I really think ——that what I'm doing is useful."

She spoke with an earnestness that struck him as odd.

"Of course it's useful. I don't doubt it."

"This place was in a mess, an incredible mess. I've had a terrific job getting it on its feet again."

"You're a good administrator. I can see that. You've got personality. You can manage people. Yes, I'm sure that you've done a much-needed and useful job here. Has it been fun?"

"Fun?"

Her startled eyes looked at him.

"It's not a word in a foreign language. It could be fun —if you loved them."

"Loved who?"

"The children."

She said slowly and sadly:

"No, I don't love them—not really—not in the way you mean. I wish I did. But then—"

"But then it would be pleasure, not duty. That's what you were thinking, wasn't it? And duty is what you must have."

"Why should you think that?"

"Because it's written all over you. Why, I wonder?"

He got up suddenly and walked restlessly up and down.

"What have you been doing all your life? It's so baffling, so extraordinary, to know you so well and to know nothing at all about you. It's—it's heart-rending. I don't know where to begin.

His distress was so real that she could only stare.

"I must seem quite mad to you. You don't understand. How should you? But I came to this country to meet you."

"To bring me Shirley's things?"

He waved an impatient hand.

"Yes, yes, that's all I thought it was. To do an errand that Richard hadn't got the heart to do. I'd no idea—not the faintest—that it would be *you*."

He leaned across the desk towards her.

"Listen, Laura, you've got to know some time—you might as well know now. Years ago, before I started on my mission, I saw three scenes. In my father's family there's a tradition of second sight. I suppose I have it too. I saw three things as clearly as I see you now. I saw an office desk, and a big-jowled man behind it. I saw a window looking out on pine trees against the sky and a man with a round pink face and an owlish expression. In due course I met and lived through those scenes. The man behind the big desk was the multi-millionaire who financed our religious crusade. Later I lay in a sanatorium bed, and I looked at those snow-covered pine trees against the sky, and a doctor with a round pink face stood by my bed and told me that my life and mission as an evangelist were over.

"The third thing I saw was *you*. *Yes,* Laura, *you*. As distinctly as I see you now. Younger than you are now, but with the same sadness in your eyes, the same tragedy in your face. I didn't see you in any particular setting, but very faintly, like an insubstantial back-cloth, I saw a church, and after that a background of leaping flames."

"Flames?"

She was startled.

"Yes. Were you ever in a fire?"

"Once. When I was a child. But the church—what kind of a church? A Catholic church, with Our Lady in a blue cloak?"

"Nothing so definite as that. No colour—or lights. Cold grey, and—yes, a font. You were standing by a font."

He saw the colour die out of her face. Her hands went slowly to her temples.

"That means something to you, Laura. What does it mean?"

"Shirley Margaret Evelyn, in the name of the Father and the Son and the Holy Ghost . . ." Her voice trailed off.

"Shirley's christening. I was Shirley's proxy godmother. I held her, and I wanted to drop her down on the stones! I wanted her to be dead! That's what was in my mind. I wished her to be dead. And now—now—she *is* dead."

She dropped her face suddenly on her hands.

"Laura, dearest, I see—oh, I see. And the flames? That means something too?"

"I prayed. Yes, prayed. I lit a candle for my Intention. And do you know what my Intention was? I wanted Shirley to die. And now—"

"Stop, Laura. Don't go on saying that. The fire—what

happened?"

"It was the same night. I woke up. There was smoke. The house was on fire. I thought my prayer had been answered. And then I heard the baby give a queer little cry, and then suddenly it was all different. The only thing I wanted was to get her out safe. And I did. She wasn't even singed. I got her out on to the grass. And then I found it was all gone—the jealousy, the wanting to be first—all gone, and I loved her, loved her terribly. I've loved her ever since."

"My dear—oh! my dear."

Again he leaned across the desk towards her.

He said urgently:

"You do see, don't you, that my coming here—"

He was interrupted as the door opened.

Miss Harrison came in breathlessly:

"The specialist is here—Mr. Bragg. He's in A ward, and is asking for you."

Laura rose.

"I'll come at once." Miss Harrison withdrew, and Laura said hurriedly:

"I'm sorry. I must go now. If you'll arrange to send me Shirley's things . . ."

"I'd rather you came to dine with me at my hotel. It's the 'Windsor,' near Charing Cross Station. Can you come to-night?"

"I'm afraid to-night's impossible."

"Then to-morrow."

"It's difficult for me to get away in the evenings—"

"You are off duty then. I've already inquired about that."

"I have other arrangements—commitments. . . ."

"It's not that. You're afraid."

"Very well then, I'm afraid."

"Of me?"

"I suppose so, yes."

"Why? Because you think I'm mad?"

"No. You're not mad. It's not that."

"But still you are afraid. Why?"

"I want to be let alone. I don't want my—my way of life disturbed. Oh! I don't know what I'm talking about. And I must go."

"But you'll dine with me—when? To-morrow? The day after? I shall wait here in London until you do."

"To-night, then."

"And get it over!" He laughed and suddenly, to her own surprise, she laughed with him. Then, her gravity restored, she went quickly to the door. Llewellyn stood aside to let her pass, and opened the door for her.

"Windsor Hotel, eight o'clock. I'll be waiting."

Chapter two

1

Laura sat before her mirror in the bedroom of her tiny flat. There was a queer smile on her lips as she studied her face. In her right hand she held a lipstick, and she looked down now at the name engraved on the gilt case. *Fatal Apple.*

She wondered again at the unaccountable impulse that had taken her so suddenly into the luxurious perfumed interior of the shop that she passed every day.

The assistant had brought out a selection of lipsticks, trying them for her to see on the back of a slim hand with long exotic fingers and deep carmine nails.

Little smears of pink and cerise and scarlet and maroon and cyclamen, some of them hardly distinguishable from one another except by their names—such fantastic names they seemed to Laura.

Pink Lightning, Buttered Rum, Misty Coral, Quiet Pink, Fatal Apple.

It was the name that attracted her, not the colour.

Fatal Apple . . . it carried with it the suggestion of Eve, of temptation, of womanhood.

Sitting before the mirror, she carefully painted her lips.

Baldy! She thought of Baldy, pulling up bindweed and lecturing her so long ago. What had he said "Show you're a woman, hang out your flag, go after your man. . . ."

Something like that. Was that what she was doing now?

And she thought: 'Yes, it's exactly that. Just for this evening, just for this once, I want to be a woman, like other women, decking herself out, painting herself up to attract her man. I never wanted to before. I didn't think I was that kind of person. But I am, after all. Only I never knew it.'

And her impression of Baldy was so strong that she could almost fancy him standing behind her, nodding his great heavy head in approval, and saying in his gruff voice:

"That's right, young Laura. Never too late to learn."

Dear Baldy . . .

Always, all through her life, there had been Baldy, her friend. Her one true and faithful friend.

Her mind went back to his deathbed, two years ago. They had sent for her, but when she had got there the doctor had explained that he was probably too far gone to recognise her. He was sinking fast and was only semi-conscious.

She had sat beside him, holding his gnarled hand between her own, watching him.

He had lain very still, grunting occasionally and puffing as though some inner exasperation possessed him. Muttered words came fitfully from his lips.

Once he opened his eyes, looked at her without recognition and said: "Where *is* the child? Send for her, can't you? And don't talk tommy-rot about its being bad for her to see anyone die. Experience, that's all . . . And children take death in their stride, better than we do."

She had said:

"I'm here, Baldy. I'm here."

But closing his eyes he had only murmured indignantly:

"Dying, indeed? I'm not dying. Doctors are all alike—gloomy devils. I'll show him."

And then he had relapsed into his half-waking state, with the occasional murmur that showed where his mind

212

was wandering, amongst the memories of his life.

"Damned fool—no historical sense . . ." Then a sudden chortle! "Old Curtis and his bone meal. My roses better than his any day."

Then her name came.

"Laura—ought to get her a dog. . . ."

That puzzled her. A dog? Why a dog?

Then, it seemed, he was speaking to his housekeeper:

"—and clear away all that disgusting sweet stuff—all right for a child—makes me sick to look at it. . . ."

Of course—those sumptuous teas with Baldy, that had been such an event of her childhood. The trouble that he had taken. The éclairs, the meringues, the macaroons . . . Tears came into her eyes.

And then suddenly his eyes were open, and he was looking at her, recognising her, speaking to her. His tone was matter of fact:

"You shouldn't have done it, young Laura," he said reprovingly. "You shouldn't have done it, you know. It will only lead to trouble."

And in the most natural manner in the world, he had turned his head slightly on his pillow and had died.

Her friend . . .

Her only friend.

Once again Laura looked at her face in the mirror. She was startled, now, at what she saw. Was it only the dark crimson line of the lipstick outlining the curve of her lips? Full lips—nothing really ascetic about them. Nothing ascetic about her in this moment of studying herself.

She spoke, half aloud, arguing with someone who was herself and yet not herself.

"Why shouldn't I try to look beautiful? Just this once? Just for to-night? I know it's too late, but why shouldn't I know what it feels like. Just to have something to remember. . . ."

2

He said at once: "What's happened to you?"

She returned his gaze equably. A sudden shyness had invaded her, but she concealed it. To regain her poise, she studied him critically.

She liked what she saw. He was not young—actually he looked older than his years (which she knew from the Press accounts of him)—but there was a boyish awkwardness about him that struck her as both strange and oddly endearing. He showed an eagerness allied with timidity, a queer, hopeful expressiveness, as though the world and everything in it was fresh and new to him.

"Nothing's happened to me." She let him help her off with her coat.

"Oh, but it has. You're different—quite different—from what you were this morning!"

She said brusquely: "Lipstick and make-up, that's all!"

He accepted her word for it.

"Oh, I see. Yes, I did think your mouth was paler than most women's usually are. You looked rather like a nun."

"Yes—yes—I suppose I did."

"You look lovely now, really lovely. You *are* lovely, Laura. You don't mind my saying so?"

She shook her head. "I don't mind."

'Say it often,' her inner self was crying. 'Say it again and again. It's all I shall ever have.'

"We're having dinner up here—in my sitting-room. I thought you'd prefer it. But perhaps—you don't mind?"

He looked at her anxiously.

"I think it's perfect."

"I hope the dinner will be perfect. I'm rather afraid it won't. I've never thought much about food until now, but I would like it to be just right for you."

She smiled at him as she sat down at the table, and he rang for the waiter.

She felt as though she was taking part in a dream.

For this wasn't the man who had come to see her this morning at the Foundation. This was a different man altogether. A younger man, callow, eager, unsure of himself, desperately anxious to please. She thought suddenly: 'This was what he was like when he was in his twenties.

This is something he's missed—and he's gone back into the past to find it.'

For a moment sadness, desperation, swept over her. This wasn't real. This was a might-have-been that they were acting out together. This was young Llewellyn and young Laura. It was ridiculous and rather pathetic, unsubstantial in time, but oddly sweet.

They dined. The meal was mediocre, but neither of them noticed it. Together they were exploring the *Pays du Tendre*. They talked, laughed, hardly noticed what they said.

Then, when the waiter finally left, setting coffee on the table, Laura said:

"You know about me—a good deal, anyway, but I know nothing about you. Tell me."

He told her, describing his youth, his parents and his upbringing.

"Are they still alive?"

"My father died ten years ago, my mother last year."

"Were they—was she—very proud of you?"

"My father, I think, disliked the form my mission took. Emotional religion repelled him, but he accepted, I think, that there was no other way for me. My mother understood better. She was proud of my world fame—mothers are—but she was sad."

"Sad?"

"Because of the things—the human things—that I was missing. And because my lack of them separated me from other human beings; and, of course, from her."

"Yes. I see that."

She thought about it. He went on, telling her his story, a fantastic story it seemed to her. The whole thing was outside her experience, and in some ways it revolted her. She said:

"It's terribly commercial."

"The machinery? Oh yes."

She said: "If only I could understand better. I want

to understand. You feel—you felt—that it was really important, really worthwhile."

"To God?"

She was taken aback.

"No—no, I didn't mean that. I meant—to *you*."

He sighed.

"It's so hard to explain. I tried to explain to Richard Wilding. The question of whether it was worthwhile never arose. It was a thing I had to do."

"And suppose you'd just preached to an empty desert, would that have been the same?"

"In my sense, yes. But I shouldn't have preached so well, of course." He grinned. "An actor can't act well to an empty house. An author needs people to read his books. A painter needs to show his pictures."

"You sound—that's what I can't understand—as though the *results* didn't interest you."

"I have no means of knowing what the results were."

"But the figures, the statistics, the converts—all those things were listed and put down in black and white."

"Yes, yes, I know. But that's machinery again, human calculations. I don't know the results that God wanted, or what he got. But understand this, Laura: if, out of all the millions who came to hear me, God wanted one—just one—soul, and chose that means to reach that soul, it would be enough."

"It sounds like taking a steam-hammer to crack a nut."

"It does, doesn't it, by human standards? That's always our difficulty, of course; we have to apply human standards of values—or of justice and injustice—to God. We haven't, can't have, the faintest knowledge of what God really requires from man, except that it seems highly probable that God requires man to become something that he could be, but hasn't thought of being yet."

Laura said:

"And what about you? What does God require of you—now?"

"Oh—just to be an ordinary sort of guy. Earn my living, marry a wife, raise a family, love my neighbours."

"And you'll be satisfied—with that?"

"Satisfied? What else should I want? What more should any man want? I'm handicapped, perhaps. I've lost fifteen years—of ordinary life. That's where you'll have to help me, Laura."

"I?"

"You know that I want to marry you, don't you? You realise, you must realise, that I love you."

She sat, very white, looking at him. The unreality of their festive dinner was over. They were themselves now. Back in the now and here that they had made for themselves.

She said slowly: "It's impossible."

He answered her without due concern: "Is it? Why?"

"I can't marry you."

"I'll give you time to get used to the idea."

"Time will make no difference."

"Do you mean that you could never learn to love me? Forgive me, Laura, but I don't think that's true. I think that, already, you love me a little."

Emotion rose up in her like a flame.

"Yes, I could love you. I do love you. . . ."

He said very softly: "That's wonderful, Laura . . . dearest Laura, my Laura."

She thrust out a hand, as though to hold him away from her.

"But I can't marry you. I can't marry anybody."

He stared at her hard.

"What's in your head? There's something."

"Yes. There's something."

"Vowed to good works? To celibacy?"

"No, no, *no!*"

"Sorry. I spoke like a fool. Tell me, my dearest."

"Yes. I must tell you. It's a thing I thought I should never tell anybody."

"Perhaps not. But you must certainly tell me."

She got up and went over to the fireplace. Without looking at him, she began to speak in a quiet matter-of-fact voice.

"Shirley's first husband died in my house."

"I know. She told me."

"Shirley was out that evening. I was alone in the house with Henry. He had sleeping-tablets, quite a heavy dose, every night. Shirley called back to me when she went out that she had given him his tablets, but I had gone back into the house. When I came, at ten o'clock, to see if he wanted anything, he told me that he hadn't had his evening dose of tablets. I fetched them and gave them to him. Actually, he *had* had his tablets—he'd got sleepy and confused, as people often do with that particular drug, and imagined that he hadn't had them. The double dose killed him."

"And you feel responsible?"

"I was responsible."

"Technically, yes."

"More than technically. I *knew* that he had taken his dose. I heard when Shirley called to me."

"Did you know that a double dose would kill him?"

"I knew that it might."

She added deliberately:

"I hoped that it would."

"I see." Llewellyn's manner was quiet, unemotional. "He was incurable, wasn't he? I mean, he would definitely have been a cripple for life."

"It was not a mercy killing, if that is what you mean."

"What happened about it?"

"I took full responsibility. I was not blamed. The question arose as to whether it might have been suicide—that is, whether Henry might have deliberately told me that he had not had his dose in order to get a second one. The tablets were never left within his reach, owing to his extravagant fits of despair and rage."

"What did you say to that suggestion?"

"I said that I did not think that it was likely. Henry

would never have thought of such a thing. He would have gone on living for years—years, with Shirley waiting on him and enduring his selfishness and bad temper, sacrificing all her life to him. I wanted her to be happy, to have her life and live it. She'd met Richard Wilding not long before. They'd fallen in love with each other."

"Yes, she told me."

"She might have left Henry in the ordinary course of events. But a Henry ill, crippled, dependent upon her—*that* Henry she would never leave. Even if she no longer cared for him, she would never have left him. Shirley was loyal, she was the most loyal person I've ever known. Oh, can't you see? I couldn't bear her whole life to be wasted, ruined. I didn't care what they did to me."

"But actually they didn't do anything to you."

"No. Sometimes—I wish they had."

"Yes, I dare say you do feel like that. But there's nothing really they could do. Even if it wasn't a mistake, if the doctor suspected some merciful impulse in your heart, or even an unmerciful one, he would know that there was no case, and he wouldn't be anxious to make one. If there had been any suspicion of Shirley having done it, it would have been a different matter."

"There was never any question of that. A maid actually heard Henry say to me that he hadn't had his tablets and ask me to give them to him."

"Yes, it was all made easy for you—very easy." He looked up at her. "How do you feel about it now?"

"I wanted Shirley to be free to—"

"Leave Shirley out of it. This is between you and Henry. How do you feel about Henry? That it was all for the best?"

"*No.*"

"Thank God for that."

"Henry didn't want to die. I killed him."

"Do you regret?"

"If you mean—would I do it again?—yes."

"Without remorse?"

"Remorse? Oh yes. It was a wicked thing to do. I know that. I've lived with it ever since. I can't forget."

"Hence the Foundation for Sub-Normal Children? Good works? A course of duty, stern duty. It's your way of making amends."

"It's all I *can* do."

"Is it any use?"

"What do you mean? It's worthwhile."

"I'm not talking of its use to others. Does it help *you?*"

"I don't know. . . ."

"It's punishment you want, isn't it?"

"I want, I suppose, to make amends."

"To whom? Henry? But Henry's dead. And from all I've heard, there's nothing that Henry would care less about than sub-normal children. You must face it, Laura, *you can't make amends."*

She stood motionless for a moment, like one stricken. Then she flung back her head, the colour rose in her cheeks. She looked at him defiantly, and his heart leapt in sudden admiration.

"That's true," she said. "I've been trying, perhaps, to dodge that. You've shown me that I can't. I told you I didn't believe in God, but I do, really. I know that what I've done was evil. I think I believe, in my heart of hearts, that I shall be damned for it. Unless I repent—and I don't repent. I did what I did with my eyes open. I wanted Shirley to have her chance, to be happy, and she *was* happy. Oh, I know it didn't last long—only three years. But if for three years she was happy and contented, and even if she did die young, then it's worth it."

As he looked at her, the greatest temptation of his life came to Llewellyn—the temptation to hold his tongue, never to tell her the truth. Let her keep her illusion, since it was all she had. He loved her. Loving her, how could he strike her brave courage down into the dust? She need never know.

He walked over to the window, pulled aside the curtain, stared out unseeing into the lighted streets.

When he turned, his voice was harsh.

"Laura," he said, "do you know how your sister died?"

"She was run over—"

"That, yes. But how she came to be run over—that you don't know. She was drunk."

"Drunk?" she repeated the word almost uncomprehendingly. "You mean—there had been a party?"

"No party. She crept secretly out of the house and down to the town. She did that now and again. She sat in a café there, drinking brandy. Not very often. Her usual practice was to drink at home. Lavender water and eau-de-Cologne. She drank them until she passed out. The servants knew; Wilding didn't."

"Shirley—drinking? But she never drank? Not in that way! Why?"

"She drank because she found her life unbearable, she drank to escape."

"I don't believe you."

"It's true. She told me herself. When Henry died, she became like someone who had lost their way. That's what she was—a lost, bewildered child."

"But she loved Richard, and Richard loved her."

"Richard loved her, but did she ever love him? A brief infatuation—that's all it ever was. And then, weakened by sorrow and the long strain of looking after an irascible invalid, she married him."

"And she wasn't happy. I still can't believe it."

"How much did you know about your sister? Does a person ever seem the same to two different people? You see Shirley always as the helpless baby that you rescued from fire, you see her as weak, helpless, in need always of love, of protection. But I see her quite differently, although I may be just as wrong as you were. I see her as a brave, gallant, adventurous young woman, able to take knocks, able to hold her own, needing difficulties to bring out the full capabilities of her spirit. She was tired and strained, but she was winning her battle, she was making a good job of her chosen life, she was bringing Henry out of despair into the daylight, she was triumphant that night that he died. She loved Henry, and Henry was what she wanted; her life was difficult, but passionately worthwhile.

"And then Henry died, and she was shoved back—back into layers of cotton-wool and soft wrapping, and anxious love, and she struggled and she couldn't get free. It was then that she found that drink helped. It dimmed reality. And once drink has got a hold on a woman, it isn't easy to give it up."

"She never told me she wasn't happy—never."

"She didn't want you to know that she was unhappy."

"And *I* did that to her—*I?*"

"Yes, my poor child."

"Baldy knew," Laura said slowly. "That's what he meant when he said: 'You shouldn't have done it, young Laura.' Long ago, long ago he warned me. *Don't interfere.* Why do we think we know what's best for other people?" Then she wheeled sharply towards him. "She didn't—mean to? It wasn't suicide?"

"It's an open question. It could be. She stepped off the pavement straight in front of the lorry. Wilding, in his heart of hearts, thinks it was."

"No. Oh, no!"

"But *I* don't think so. I think better of Shirley than that. I think she was often very near to despair, but I don't believe she ever really abandoned herself to it. I think she was a fighter, I think she continued to fight. But you don't give up drinking in the snap of a finger. You relapse every now and then. I think she stepped off that pavement into eternity without knowing what she was doing or where she was going."

Laura sank down on to the sofa.

"What shall I do? Oh! What shall I do?"

Llewellyn came and put his arms round her.

"You will marry me. You'll start again."

"No, no, I can never do that."

"Why not? You need love."

"You don't understand. I've got to pay. For what I've done. Everyone has to pay."

"How obsessed you are by the thought of payment."

Laura reiterated: "Everyone has to pay."

"Yes, I grant you that. But don't you see, my dearest child—" He hesitated before this last bitter truth that she had to know. "For what you did, someone has already paid. *Shirley paid.*"

She looked at him in sudden horror.

"Shirley paid—for what I did?"

He nodded.

"Yes. I'm afraid you've got to live with that. Shirley paid. And Shirley is dead, and the debt is cancelled. You have got to go forward, Laura. You have got, not to forget the past, but to keep it where it belongs, in your memory, but not in your daily life. You have got to accept not punishment but happiness. Yes, my dear, happiness. You have got to stop giving and learn to take. God deals strangely with us—He is giving you, so I fully believe, happiness and love. Accept them in humility."

"I can't. I can't!"

"You must."

He drew her to her feet.

"I love you, Laura, and you love me—not as much as I love you, but you do love me."

"Yes, I love you."

He kissed her—a long, hungry kiss.

As they drew apart, she said, with a faint shaky laugh: "I wish Baldy knew. He'd be pleased!"

As she moved away, she stumbled and half fell.

Llewellyn caught her.

"Be careful—did you hurt yourself?—you might have struck your head on that marble chimney-piece."

"Nonsense."

"Yes, nonsense—but you're so precious to me. . . ."

She smiled at him. She felt his love and his anxiety.

She was wanted, as in her childhood she had longed to be wanted.

And suddenly, almost imperceptibly, her shoulders sagged a little, as though a burden, a light burden, but still a burden, had been placed on them.

For the first time, she felt and comprehended the weight of love. . . .

Classic Tales by the Mistress of Mystery

AGATHA CHRISTIE